the Singing men
and
other stories

Derek Gregory

introduction by
Mark Adlard

first published October 2002 by IRON Press
5 Marden Terrace
Cullercoats
Northumberland
NE30 4PD
England
tel/fax:+44 (0)191 253 1901
Email: seaboy@freenetname.co.uk
web site: www.ironpress.co.uk

ISBN 0 906228 86 7

printed by
Peterson Printers, South Shields

© stories, Derek Gregory Estate 2002
© introduction Mark Adlard

typset in Trebuchet MS10pt

Cover and Book design by
IRON Eye Design @ IRON Press

IRON Press books are available to trade from
Central Books

the stories

7
Singing Men

12
Astronomy

16
Bag Lady

21
Bubbles

27
Executive Toy

33
Last Train from Lodz

38
Long Blond Hair

41
Lucinda Says

47
Pig

59
Reec-Ret

68
Water Baby

73
The New Queen

79
Tell me About Pierre

88
Death of a Gasholder

96
The Launching

Acknowledgements

Some of these stories have been previously
published or broadcast as follows:

Astronomy - The European
Lucinda Says - BBC Radio 4
Water Babies - Panurge Magazine
Death of a Gasholder - Northern Tales
(winner of Sid Chaplin Short Story Competition)
The Singing Men - winner of the Greyfriars Literary Comp.
The Launching - IRON Magazine

MARK ADLARD

Mark Adlard wrote the *Tcity Trilogy,* which comprises three
novels: *Interface* (1971), *Volteface* (1972) and *Multiface* (l975).
The action takes place in a huge future city which
occupies the North East coast of England.
The Greenlander (1978) is an historical novel
whose background is the whaling industry of Whitby.

INTRODUCTION

Derek Gregory is probably best remembered at present as the editor of the *Tees Valley Writer*. This magazine appeared twice a year and provided scores of aspiring writers with the opportunity of appearing in print for the first time, as well as supplying a platform for those already established. Hundreds of writers have continued to lament its disappearance.

Derek was born on May 20, 1928, in Hunslet, one of the tougher parts of Leeds. His father was a labourer on a public works project, but later was lucky enough to obtain a job which required him to go round with a bag collecting gas metre payments. Unfortunately the weight of all those pennies damaged his back irreparably. His mother was an outworker for Montagu Burton, the tailor, but only part-time. Like many such boys who were clever without knowing it, Derek left school early as a matter of course, and took a number of dead-end jobs.

He discovered literature and his first intellectual pleasures of any kind, while doing National Service. It was an awakening he always recalled with profound gratitude. He soon developed a voracious thirst for knowledge, began to study seriously for the first time, and eventually went on to obtain a BA in Economics from Leeds Univerisity, followed some years later by an MA. I happened to see an official envelope addressed to him, and discovered he also had a Ph.D from York. By far his most successful publication was *Statistics for Business*, published by McGraw Hill, which ran to four editions.

When I first met Derek Gregory he was teaching at Teesside Polytechnic. That was the start of our friendship, the precursor to many convivial meetings and excursions with our wives. I say 'many', but I shall always regret not having struck up a friendship with him earlier, so that there could have been many, many more. Within days, Derek became one of my closest friends and he enriched my life. Characters in a couple of the following stories are troubled by angina pains. Derek Gregory was, it hardly needs saying, very well read; and he was very well informed, which isn't the same thing. He was familiar with the general history of all the arts, not just literature. He played the clarinet and timpani in an orchestra. He was a skilful gardener and had a very large and beautiful garden to prove it. He was an excellent cook, always ready to try out a new recipe on his guests, and regularly drank copious amounts of wine without paying much attention to the label. He was very funny in an unemphatic ironic sort of way.

I knew that he wrote short stories, because I had come across two or three by chance. He was always immensely self-effacing to the point of avoiding people who would have liked to meet him. He never mentioned his work until the day he couldn't resist telling me that he had won a £1000 prize which would be put into his hand by Moira Shearer. ("Of course", he said, with his characteristic smile, "nowadays we just call her Moira"). I told him that perhaps he would accumulate enough stories to publish a collection. The usual smile. I never thought I should become the instigator of such a collection.

Derek's widow, Jennifer, showed me a drawer that contained sufficient stories to furnish several collections. I felt like Howard Carter. Some of the stories had been published, but most had not. There was much evidence of constant rewriting to improve structure and eliminate stale language. Sometimes I could identify a personal experience, and occasionally I imagined that I had made an unwitting contribution. There was a fascination with the ghastly or the morbid which I had not expected. Almost all the stories were of high quality, and some of them absolutely dazzling. I wish I had known about them earlier.

Each story has what appears to be its particular theme - a variety of subjects that include pig-breeding, lost love, a day in the life of a sales rep., nursery school, a train from Poland to Germany in the 30s, a steam cruise, a dam in Africa. There is a lightly-worn expertise and specialist knowledge which are never paraded or displayed for their own sake, but only as required by the needs of the story. The stories are animated by a series of characters who monopolise our attention as they express (or try to express) themselves in their idiosyncratic ways. The characters are often obsessed - by childlessness, wine-making, a little girl, bees, water. Derek had a wonderful ear for the inanities of dialogue.

Derek Gregory's world is a menacing place. 'Nature' is identified not as a source of morality and goodness, as in Wordsworth, but of cruelty and evil, as in Leopardi. Our sins, our folly and our obsessions, make a bad situation worse and drive us into 'corridors of terror and magic.' Even when we try to remedy the casual cruelty of the world, some inscrutable power mocks our striving.
But all is not lost. We have the transforming power of words, and the use of words in these stories is a continuing delight: Here you will be regarded by eyes as cold as a witch's teat; you will see the dried snakeskins of river beds; you will come across a children's author who floods her jaw with gin. Our humdrum environment is touched by poetry: a man in a hypermarket reflects that anybody accidentally locked in "could survive perhaps for years, glimpsing the sky through the distant windows and sensing the wind by the blown litter hammering at the automatic doors."

And we have humour. If a story such as *Pig* did not make you laugh, it would be unbearable.

And we can dare to be kind in an unkind universe. Derk Gregory's detached view of human foibles is undercut by a pervasise sympathy for those whose lives are defective, even when this is due to their own foolishness. He would like to help them if he could, just as he tried to help people in what we regard as real life.

Mark Adlard
September 2002

The Singing Men

My Auntie Minnie had a large black varnished bun on the back of her head. Her great arms put me in mind of Popeye's but hers cradled a bosom which projected like a sweet counter at Woolworths. Her middle regions took the shape of a bundle of hastily assembled washing. I don't think I ever looked any further down. I had plenty of opportunity because we all lived in the same street for years. Up to the age of eight I assumed she was solid from the ankles up.

Well, that was my Auntie Minnie. Now for Uncle Joe. Yes, you've guessed - a little man. But he *was!* Why did big women marry little men in those days? It wasn't just on seaside postcards. Or did women grow bigger and men start shrinking after marriage?

Uncle Joe did. He lost his leg whilst working in an engineering factory in Leeds. He lost it because of smoking. I found it hard to believe that a leg could have anything to do with smoking. Anyway he stopped smoking after that and started singing. The leg was quite a blow because Uncle was always a bit of a dandy, but he'd also lost the tops of two fingers in a lathe accident. Life seemed to be scraping bits of him away as it passed by, whilst Auntie only grew bigger. In his youth he had a malacca cane and he wore spats and hair oil. That was why Auntie married him.

He was a thin, jittery person. She was a ruminant person. She must have been fascinated by his darting body which vibrated like a vagrant wind rattling through a ginnell. They remained together until death parted them for three whole days, one from the other.

Giving up his cigarettes was bad for Joe. They were part of his persona. He did tricks with them. The cigarette would be stuck in the corner of his mouth, the ash growing longer. Then, when the tension became unbearable he would blow off the fragile grey finger without removing it. He did several other things with a cigarette. When it got to less than halfway, he could grip it between his bottom teeth and lower lip and make it disappear into his mouth. He would stare at you, crazily marbled eyes popping with hot torture, and then regurgitate it with a retching motion. Another trick was throwing it up into his mouth straight from the packet. I believe I once saw Humphrey Bogart do exactly the same years later. Perhaps he was copying off Uncle Joe. You can see why my Uncle missed his smoking. It also meant him giving up his spats. You can't wear spats on one foot.

As I say, after he stopped smoking he started singing, probably to take his mind off smoking. Though in moments of nervous concentration he would curl his tongue from the corner of his mouth, like a cow trying to lick its nostrils. I expect this was a kind of cigarette substitute. But between the smoking and the singing came the alcohol. He never drank to excess. He just made wine to excess, though drinking some of it must have improved his fine natural baritone voice.

He joined the church choir without any thoughts of God, merely to impress others (as small men often do). Though he went to church he refused to become a church member. His interest was only in singing. The vicar tried his best. He pointed out the benefits of Salvation and other tempting inducements. He described how in the Bible water was miraculously turned into wine. Uncle Joe, unimpressed, said he performed that one every evening in the cellar. The vicar, recently ordained, was far too intellectual for either of them. He tackled Auntie Minnie, who was quite innocent of any logic other than her own. One winter's day as he sat on her hot plum velvet sofa he asked conversationally, "Why is it, Mrs Webster, that you put bacon rind in the mouse trap? I thought the little creatures preferred cheese?" She never looked up from the cellar-head where she spiked the trap with the remains of Joe's breakfast. "Because it's better for their little chests." Henceforth the vicar reserved his pastoral beliefs for more fertile vineyards.

Unlike my parents, Auntie Minnie and Uncle Joe did things. For example, every Saturday in summer they set off into alien countryside on Uncle's ancient motorbike to gather fruit and blossoms for wine-making. When Auntie was fully stuffed into the sidecar I used to envy her the privacy and comfort, sealed in that bobbing perspex torpedo. Later, when I built balsa-wood models of Stuka dive-bombers I was always reminded of Auntie like a pilot, blinking at the world through the windscreen.

They hadn't any children. There were whispers of a golden-haired treasure who had flitted through life as far as her second month. Auntie mentioned her once in an unguarded moment as she stared into the sockets of the fire over a bottle of Joe's cowslip wine. When I told Mum she just sniffed and said anybody could have children. They never really *wanted* them. She may have been jealous because, having gone through the labour of childbirth with so many us, we went round to Auntie's to play out the rest of our lives. Auntie loved all children and was, in her blissful milky manner, almost one of them.

If tramps loitered on the cobbles outside, she stood sentinel at the window. She made an exception for wounded men from the First World War who came round singing for money. They lasted right until the Second World War. Many had only one leg, like Uncle. She had no money to give to them, but the sympathy radiated from her house. And Joe, decanting his wine in the cellar would break off practising next Sunday's hymn to join them in a chorus of *Red Sails in the Sunset*. His booming would echo up through the cellar grating and startle the poor war veterans. I would step out in the street on these occasions and join them trailing a few steps behind. I adored singing as much as Uncle Joe. Frequently, the singing men, suspicious of being mocked, would speed up at the end of a verse and, without losing tempo, turn around and unleash a savage but low-pitched string of swear words at me. Auntie frequently rushed out with a penny to restore a poor man's confidence in himself.

Of course, in the early thirties there would be gangs of singing men in our street. Mostly they wore medals and they carried triangles and tambourines to emphasise the rhythm of their songs. It was easier for me to join a singing group. They usually ended up round Auntie's front door sipping hot soup.

When the depression was at its height Auntie started a small shop. No babies must have meant a great gap in her life and as we grew older we spent more time at home with arithmetic and essays. Her learning only amounted to writing the odd message. Figures? Yes. Words? No chance. The shop gave her an interest. She opened it by simply moving the aspidistra and replacing the sash window with a larger one. Scales on the counter and a tinkly bell on the door quickly followed. It was a corner 'through' house with the use of a privy in either street. At the back door she sold bulky goods, buckets of coal, firewood and bagged flour and sugar. She was so successful that the coalman resented her enterprise and finished by hardly coming down our street with his horse-drawn cart. Much to the intense disappointment of those with allotments. The Co-op manager muttered resentfully when she took in Uncle's boots for repair. Whilst other women managed the midwife's job or prepared the dead for burial she became a universal provider and a one-woman relief organisation for the street during the slump.

Part of her secret was her tick-book. Her accounts were meticulous. Her Christmas Club started in the New year, her holiday club after Wakes Week. She means-tested her customers like the Public Assistance, but with a woman's touch and a more intimate knowledge of their circumstances.

In just over a year she had bought the house next door and knocked the wall through. Wagging tongues said she was too well-off because she had no babies, but I put it down to creative accounting. Of course this meant more cellar space for Uncle's wine. The number of fermenting flagons under the shop gave out a regular throb. The aroma in the shop amounted to virtually imbibing when you took a breath. They used to say if you lit a ciggy down my Uncle's cellar the carbon dioxide would snuff it out before you could take a drag. The coalman said it, and the gasman when he came to read the meter. So did the electric man. All these people who supplied my Auntie with fuel and power had their cigarettes extinguished when they opened the cellar door, though they enjoyed the smell and the singing.

It wasn't long before she bought the house on the other side. Finally she had to take male advice on load-bearing walls and reinforced joists. All this time Uncle was merrily laying down bottles in a squirrel-like way. Much of it required years to mature. The question of who was going to drink it hardly seemed to bother him. Probably he had visions of their old age when the physical activity might give way to an extensive rosy, chair bound, stupor.

Before the war Auntie started a créche for the street, anticipating government action by about fifty years. As our own family had grown Mother willingly let me attend until the time came to go to the big school. Perhaps I got too used to the heady scent of the Auntie's. At all events I returned from the second day at the big school to announce that I wouldn't be going again, as the teacher had simply repeated what we did on day one. This statement shocked Auntie, but apparently no-one else. Mother tore me screaming from Auntie's bosomy grasp. I had served my babyhood.

During the Second World War everything seemed to change. I grew into a little snob after the School Certificate and despised the street I grew up in. Singing men ceased to interest me. My Uncle had grown even smaller, as did the whole street. He sang less, and Auntie grew more vexed with ration coupons and the need to fill in official returns. There were rumours of black market activities, of suspect

Irishmen and foreigners. The war seemed to bring out the worse in everybody.

Uncle Joe was too old for the Forces, of course, but able to make a lot of money in overtime at the engineering works. He combined this with tuneful stretches of fire-watching. The money he saved gave him an income he could not have dreamed of before the war. Auntie continued to buy property in the street, untempted by the new pre-war housing estates. She had a whole shop frontage built covering four houses. This meant more property to tunnel through and more cellarage space for Uncle's wine. She launched into lino and fancy goods, with assistants to serve in the evenings. They never lived to inhabit those comfortable, boring, fireside chairs. Uncle died of cirrhosis a few years after the war ended. Auntie lingered for a few more days sipping his cowslip wine which she loved.

When we went to straighten out their effects it was clear she had been a wartime hoarder. Most of the rooms upstairs were shored up with great columns of half-rusted tins which had lost their labels. "I *expected* something like this!" Mother snorted. For a time we had a great deal of fun opening tins just before each meal. Sometimes we had tinned spam for tea, closely followed by dressed crab and dried egg. Then again it might be pineapple chunks with pilchards, washed down, of course, with vintage cowslip.

After a time this palled. Tea grew too unpredictable. We were living in the suburbs on a development and the old street became part of the council's structure plan. The demolition men moved in and we left the rest of the wine where it was, in the honeycomb of the cellars. By now a completely different set of people had taken over part of the street, the type who Auntie would have crossed over the road in to avoid.

The demolition men took more time over that street than the rest of the area. They were frequently found asleep on the job and had difficulty in lighting their cigarettes. The terrace of houses was permitted to stand until everywhere else was demolished. For a while it seemed as though it would survive. Ragged flags of wallpaper fluttered on the walls. A cast-iron bedroom fireplace stared down, its throat gaping. Then they came down, the flat acres of cheap brick ruins frosted with broken bottles as the crash of the great swinging metal ball beat a rhythm to the chorus of happy singing men. I always felt that that street was a woman's street, that men were visitors, like birds which perch and sing cheerfully between their wild journeys.

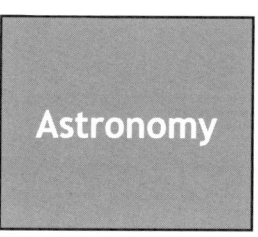

Astronomy

He looked back at the black web fissured by the sword of Orion. Away from the promenade lights the stars seemed to spring out like press studs. It didn't seem that far.

Then he went into the hotel, to the room he had specially asked for. It brought back the smell of dust that crawled away from daylight. He unpacked the suit and hung it in the wardrobe to iron later. It had to be crease-free or people would get the wrong impression. Besides, it had to go back by the weekend.

He put the recording gear under the bed, then laid his length on the counterpane, boots on the foot board. The ornaments stared at him from the mantlepiece. He had this fantastic memory but he wouldn't have recognised the room without knowing. He remembered it big. But he was only six and everything seemed big, even the stairs which had bent his knees like hairgrips. It was the only time Rose ever had money for a holiday, except for a quarter day excursion to Scarborough just after she was married.

He pulled the scuffed postcard from his pocket. It said on the back *"Summer (ha, ha) 1969, Dear Ada, Glad your not here at Sandcar with me and Arthur. Its being raining all week worse than back in old Ireland, Love,* Rose." On the front was a photo of a parade of boarding houses and an arrow pointing to a bedroom window with a message, *"Our glory hole!"*

After a bit, he had a wash and broke into a new packet of cigarettes. Then he went downstairs. The woman at the reception desk was watching something on a tiny portable telly. She gave him a streaky bacon smile.

He went into the lobby and signed the Visitors' Book. Then he looked up and saw the sign was still there. "Definitely no sand inside the hotel". Rose had pointed it out one day when it had stopped raining long enough for them to make a dash for the beach.

"See what it says? 'No sand in the hotel.' Mind you kick your shoes on the step when you come in." The landlady stood in the vestibule smiling, approving of the spoken warning as much as the conspiracy to call it a hotel.

As he walked down the prom the wind knifed into his legs. The breath of it threw bitter smoke back into his mouth. He spit out the fag. Now where was the miniature golf course? He found it broken up into great hexagonal cakes of concrete. The hut for renting the clubs had gone. The pier itself was a shrunken defensive stub and the sea crashed joyfully over the stumps of its broken thighs. His eyes searched the crescent of the coast. What was he looking for? The Punch and Judy? The drunken tractor man who pulled up the boats? His eyes caught the swirls of people as they polarised like filings near the promenade.

Down below the gulls swooped to the blistered railings. In spite of the torch of the sun, a cool wind strafed through the coarse cliff-top grass. He blew on his hands. If he didn't get a job in the next few weeks... He thought of the children and the woman he'd left them with. Why had he come? The young cowboys were getting in on the act in the shopping malls where the biggest crowds were.

And those bloody electricity bills. He'd be giving up smoking and drinking one of these days. Swear to it. Rose told him they lived off watercress sandwiches and knuckle bacon in the thirties. Times were different now - expectations. He could just see his file at the DHSS. On top, in red, "Client given to occasional outbreaks of abuse."

He ran his hand over his shaven head. It was cold now, but his head had heated up in the helmet before he had it cut. Space man! He remembered how Rose had started him off, with a pair of plastic binoculars bought on the beach that Summer. He had stared at the tankers on the blue crayoned rim of the horizon. Then the telescope later, after he had the squint operation. Ah - astronomy! She was surprised when he had taken the drama course at university. He tried to explain that art was only science without the mumbo-jumbo.

He went back to the digs after a meal and a drink in the pub to get warm. He lay in the bed again. Honestly, it might be hopeless. He would know tomorrow on the promenade. An assessment of demand was wanted. A space probe.

If he closed his eyes he could almost think that Rose was beside him, warm and milky with softness and her sweet breath, inquisitive and questioning, with her Galway accent.

He lay and stared. Rose would have known what to do. He had

left parts of himself in many places and one of the parts was in this bedroom. He fell asleep dreaming of Rose. That Rose had married him and was looking after his children feeding them watercress and streaky bacon. When he woke after midnight, he thought he heard someone sobbing in the room. Then he dried his eyes on the sheet and slept soundly.

Next morning he took his gear downstairs in two cases. The woman in reception gave him a funny look.

"It's all right," he said. "I'm doing a show on the beach. Any case I want to pay in advance, two nights." He put down the cases and offered the money. She fingered it. He could tell she was wondering how many ornaments and things were still left in the room.

He set up the recording gear in a spot which he had noticed from the cliff-top. Several small boys came to watch as he put on the helmet. He felt the heat especially in the corrugated trunking round the elbows and knees.

When he got the helmet on he felt a different person. It jutted out over the lower jaw and the gold sprayed visor hid his eyes from observers. He felt fearless in the hot dark, heavy with loops of wire and flashing battery lights. The face was moulded in smooth plastic, grey like the body stocking, like the features of a shop dummy. It was hot like a wet suit except that it didn't cool off. The main thrill was to be like something else. Not unemployed, or on the dodge. Not freighted down with kids. Silly, really. Make-believe. Something free and pure, from another planet. Shining knight of the future bringing peace and enlightenment to Earthlings. Oh, Earthlings, I bring you...?

He put the collecting box in front of the cassette player and propped up the handwritten notice, "I am a spaceman far from home." Then he switched on the spiky plonky music. He stood stock still. Arms slightly raised from his sides.

When the crowd had collected he began. Firstly he swivelled his head, as if testing the atmosphere for a hostile environment. Then the arms came into play, locking and twisting to engage hidden cogs, then gyrating hips, then the rest of the body. His legs, stiff at first, tentative of the terrain, advanced slowly to the kerb of the prom. He stopped and his hand waved like a praying mantis. A giggling group of school girls shrank back. One of them screamed "I think it likes you Audrey!" He retreated, then came forward to a small boy who inspected him through tinned-rimmed glasses. He circled the boy as though intrigued by the alien who gripped his mother's skirt. When the tape came to an end his arms and legs clicked back into his body like a neat penknife. His head dropped lifelessly on his chest, bowed and waiting for the applause.

Afterwards in the pub he took off his helmet and sponged his head in the Gents' before he counted the money. He stowed everything in the cases except the trousers and boots which he kept on to walk back to the hotel. Dusk sharpened the promenade lights and the spring twilight sent the few trippers back for boarding house teas. Going the other way, he passed the small boy who hung on his mother's arm. The boy turned to stare at him goggle-eyed until his twisting arm reached its limit, and he was yanked forwards.

Before he went in the digs he raised his eyes to the south. Same sky. Orion was there with its three blue studs. The woman was behind the desk. He looked at the sign and carefully knocked all the sand from his space boots. He jingled the coins in his pocket. Five pounds thirty. It was no good - his space shot. He would go home tomorrow and pass the suit in.

Bag Lady

Captain Von Krump wanted to throw Mrs Comfrey overboard. Naturally we all protested and he soon caved in. To us she looked lovelier dead than alive, surrounded by all that ice. A glacial, bewitching maiden.

We boarded the ship in Hamburg, only eight of us. No ship-to-shore streamer, or anything. It was simply a dented, rusted, streaked and stained tramp steamer, a bag lady of the seas, plying for profit. But for us, as passengers, it was a cheapo cargo cruise.

Apart from his monocle, our captain sported a greasy sweater for his drink-and-drive sessions on the bridge. At our enforced eating sessions at the 'captain's table' he wore a tuxedo bearing the battle honours of a hundred meals, and underneath this an *Iron Maiden* T-shirt of hideous design.

When we mounted the gangway von Krump crushed all our hands with his handshake. But Mrs Comfrey clearly staggered him with her feather-breath charm. In his awe he simply offered his large paw as a kind of hairy altar for the delicate parcel of bird bones she proffered. It appeared that Mrs Comfrey and her husband were poets of some kind.

After greeting us, von Krump retired to the bridge and, with a single toot from its forest of pipes, the ship slunk like a stray cat from the quay-side.

No-one saw them that day or the next. We met, ate, talked, until the conversation firmly centred on the mysterious Comfreys. What did he write? What was the name behind her initial 'Z'? We would ask the purser.

"Purser is me", said von Krump.

All right then, we said, the steward.

"Steward is me also," he said with an unhappy grin.

"Is it Zelda, as in Scott Fitzgerald?" we asked.

"Is Zipporah," he replied. "As in Bible! Is Jew, I tink. Now I must go to bridge."

He usually retired to the bridge after any conversation with the passengers involving despair or elation. In moments of more extreme excitement he would polish his monocle vigorously.

It appeared that the Comfreys had come to get away from it all and to avert Zipporah Comfrey's imminent artistic mental collapse.

A Bible was brought and quickly scanned. We were all for giving up around Exodus when we spotted the name. Krump was quite right. Zipporah was the wife of Moses. After circumcising her son with a stone she seemed to drop out of the narrative.

This early successful parry of our enquiries gave von Krump some kind of status, which he proceeded to exploit savagely.

"Is Nederland!" he exclaimed triumphantly as we passed Holland on our left.

"Is English country!" he poked a marlin spike of a finger towards the starboard side. Then, exhausted by this social congress he retired to stare at us from the bridge, frequently applying a bottle to his lips.

Not until the sun shone off Portugal did the Comfreys venture on deck. By that time the six of us had achieved a level of intimacy where we were swapping sun tan lotions and, in some isolated cases, even anointing each others' whitish forms. At this stage there were a few passenger complaints and von Krump always listened with his monocle inserted and his head slumped studiously to one side. This gave him the impression of having taken a sideways headshot.

At dinner he listened attentively to the tale from our Geordie couple who were plagued by a loose bolt running wild in the bulkhead above their berths. It had probably been welded into a hollow box girder by some vengeful ship's fitter. With the pitch of the small vessel it rolled from one end to the other, they reported, "like a drunken tart doing a foxtrot." In spite of a furiously polished monocle von Krump could never penetrate their accent and he took the complaint to mean that some rodent had disturbed their sleep.

"Rats! Ve vill have none of zem!" He proclaimed, flourishing his fork above the sauerkraut.

The Comfreys were privy to none of this pantomime. They ate all meals in their cabin. We assumed this was allowed for in the cost of their passage and supplied from the huge luggage trunks which had followed them on board. The bewitching Zipporah anyway looked too exquisite to have a digestive system. She spent most of her time shuffling tarot cards and sighing into the middle distance waves. Mr Comfrey occasionally committed some passing couplet to a scented mauve pad strapped to his thigh.

We hadn't much time for him. But for Zipporah no task was too onerous: opening heavy ship's doors, struggling with recalcitrant deck-chairs and, for the more fortunate, steadying her gossamer frame against the mutinous roll of the ship. This was all men's work, of course, but amazingly the women of the group were not discomfited or even censorious. Indeed, Zipporah captivated them to such a degree that they would often urge us on to greater acts of kindness. Her thanks were veritable gifts. Her earnest heliotrope eyes would plunge into your skull and her heaven's gate smile would lift you to new sunlit uplands of consciousness. There was not one man who had not transferred to her something, however small, from the love he had previously borne his wife.

Yet, when we were hardly out of the Suez canal, Mrs Comfrey was bitten on the cheek by some kind of noxious insect. Solicitous enquiries were all tragically useless. Remedies proposed were empty of effect. Angry judgements were passed on the perfidious nature of, and lack of hygiene in, the lands beyond the sludge-brown sandbanks. The insect bite grew worse. It swelled and festered, and in days, as with the late Lord Carnarvon, Zipporah Comfrey passed un-peacefully away.

Victor Comfrey was enfeebled with grief. He threw himself on our mercy, inviting an intimacy he had denied before. We were allowed to troop past the pathetic corpse in the Comfrey cabin. Zipporah was no more than an embroidery of ethereal flesh cosseting an ugly purple wound.

Von Krump fiddled mightily with his monocle and handed round black arm bands at the dinner table. Comfrey joined us, unable to face the ghastly truth in his cabin.

After dinner we dispersed to the lounge but soon became aware of raised voices from the captain's cabin.

"I won't have her buried at sea! It's damned barbaric!"

We gathered outside the door. It was Comfrey's voice. And it was the cry of a tortured man.

"She hadn't some contagious disease, you know!"

Von Krump retorted: "Dot eez to me as Kapitan if vee bury or not."

A silence, during which we could imagine the monocle being frenziedly polished. Then, "Eez because your vife eez Juden?"

"No! Damn you! She gave up her religion when she married me. It's just that she shouldn't be fed to some bloody shark!"

"Eez for insurance ting?"

"We have no insurance, damn you!"

A pause.

"Ze death eez by food, maybe? Not insect?"

Comfrey's voice sunk low. "What the hell are you suggesting ,you rotten kraut?"

"Not suggest. Try to make ting easy for every-man."

Odd phrases slipped through... "see you get another command...", "witnesses who will vouch..." We could picture the captain's head slouching on his shoulder, his eye free from the discipline of the monocle, rolling uncontrollably.

"So you think because we didn't fancy your blasted wurst and sauerkraut I poisoned her!" Comfrey's voice reached a shriek. Then he opened the door and rushed past us. "He thinks I poisoned Zipporah and he wants to throw her overboard!" He stuttered over his shoulder.

Von Krump came through the door, saw us and spread his large hands. "Maybe zis crazy man vants to put vife on some ice until vee go to Hamburg?" He hovered, waiting for support. There was silence. "I go to bridge now!" But he stood stock still. His head wished to be on the bridge but his legs were paralyzed.

Then "It's damned barbaric just to chuck her in the ocean," the Geordie said. We thought of sharks' teeth ripping into the beautiful body. It was then that von Krumps fanciful idea found favour.

"That's it!" cried someone. "Pack it in ice till we reach port!"

The monocle fell from the captain's eye. "Vee ice haf not so much. Eez long time before vee come to port." He hesitated at our disbelieving looks. "Und zee veather is zo hot!" He tried to confirm this by flapping his arms.

"We can all make sacrifices," said the Geordie.

The captain tried again. "I haf to take cargo. Vee haf to make profit. Zee cargo eez - " he hesitated.

"Perishable?" someone suggested sarcastically.

Looking back, I think it was the word "profit" which incensed us the most. That evening von Krump had to dine alone. We made it clear we were willing to address a mass petition to the owners if he refused. That document might also refer in a pointed fashion to the cocktail lounge he laughingly called the bridge.

Comfrey came down to breakfast, his face shining.

"He's agreed to do it! The carpenters made a sort of temporary extended coffin to accommodate the ice. The cook said he'd keep it in the galley."

We were all cheered by this news. The Geordie made some reference to scotch-off-the rocks, but it soon became evident that this was not the only sacrifice we had to make.

In the days following, the small ship laboured in the troughs of the Indian Ocean, her engines running in high gear to feed the inefficient refrigeration unit. The Geordie complained the loose bolt above his bunk was now doing a quickstep. The ship's electrician ingeniously found a way to divert precious electricity from our power and lighting to feed the greedy, clanking, refrigeration unit.

At the equator the ice had to be replaced in quicker rotation. Dim lights only permitted. Radios, shaving, and boiled water were rationed. Von Krump was making us pay in blood and sweat for our efforts to put Mrs Comfrey in limbo.

When we reached the South Pacific von Krump called for water at Tahiti, and surreptitiously tried to take on a load of custard apples which he obviously intended to chill. Comfrey, who had taken to prowling the deck, accused him of putting profit before his respect for the dead. Soon a trail of abandoned fruit marked our passage round the northern tip of New Zealand, reminding us all of the incident of the breadfruit and the ill-advised truculence of the late captain Bligh.

Comfrey demanded to see his dead wife at intervals and von Krump, now as nervous as a tormented cat, insisted that we all visit the galley to prove to us that he had kept faith.

At Southampton, out of respect, Zipporah Comfrey left the ship first. From the rails we watched the body bag being transferred to a special chilled van. It seemed strange that the bag contained a lady.

Von Krump watching us from the bridge, sent down a tray of celebratory drinks. He smiled weakly and raised a bottle in a toast. Suddenly there was plenty of ice. Zipporah no longer needed our cold comfort. The ice we had sacrificed now tinkled in our glasses. As it dripped down our chins we probably felt closer to her than we had ever been on the entire voyage.

Bubbles

"We don't do crisps!" said the tall lady. "Nor fruit drinks. Milk and apple slice for breaks. Calcium and vitamins are what growing children need."

The little girl tilted her head right back and looked up at the tall lady, up the long grey dress to where a silver butterfly stuck out on her chest. The butterfly quivered when she spoke. At her last crèche Barbie had kicked the lady in the ankle and made her walk with a stick. She wouldn't do that here. This lady had thick fawn stockings which smelled of washing-up.

"Sounds OK to me, Mrs Treherne," said Barbie's mother and clicked shut her make-up mirror. "By the way it's Barbie. But we call her Bubbles!" She ruffled Barbie's golden curly hair. "It's just while I'm at work in afternoons, see?"

Barbie looked round the playroom, at the children, the sand tray in the middle and, under the window, the water tank with its blue rocking water and plastic ducks. A small girl stood beside it holding a dripping soap bottle. The girl's eyes were big as she smiled. They went watery as they met Barbie's, gleaming under her ringlets.

"Has Barbie been in crèche before?" Mrs Treherne asked.

"Could never afford it," Barbie's mother lied. "Until I got this Job." Barbie looked up at her mother. Her face was painted red and green like the painted clown faces round the walls. Barbie liked her mother because she was always bright and happy. She looked at the far wall where a burst of yellow balloons bobbed and nudged each other like chattering bubbles.

"I'd better leave a number to reach me, if there's any trouble," said Barbie's mother. She scribbled on a cigarette packet. "It's the White Swan."

Mrs Treherne took the note and read the phone number as if it was the first one she had ever seen. "I do hope Barbie will settle down," she said without blinking. "It's a fortnight's payment in advance."

When her mother had gone, Barbie went over to the small girl and watched her fill the soap bottle. Then she took it from her and went over to the sand tray. The other children stepped aside. Barbie poured the water over their sand pies. Then she went back to the water tank and pushed down the nozzle. She pumped the bottle until the bubbles mounted in a towering frothy pyramid. The small girl squealed with delight and the other children began to laugh. Barbie looked at them, each in turn. She turned again and found herself looking into fawn stockings. Her gaze went up to where the silver butterfly shuddered on Mrs Treherne's chest.

Mrs Treherne pulled the soap bottle from Barbie's hand and gave it to the small girl. Mrs Treherne seemed to be smiling very fast. "Well Barbie! Or should I call you Bubbles? I'm sure you've learned a thing or two at home. And no doubt in the streets as well." She was speaking quickly and quivering the butterfly. "I do hope we can count on your co-operation."

She went over to the door and shouted "Elsie! Hannah! Come, please!" She brought back a striped apron from a clothes peg on the wall. It had a happy face on it, a big yellow face, like a smiling full moon. Mrs Treherne thrust it over Barbie's head and brought it down sharply, scraping her face. Barbie's stomach squeezed as the strings were pulled very tightly. Mrs Treherne noticed the spreading pool round Barbie's track shoes. When Elsie and Hannah came through the door Mrs Treherne's lips were pressed like a purse.

Elsie was taller with brown screwed curls. Hannah was fat and the upper parts of her arms were small pink cushions. Mrs Treherne stared at Barbie and rubbed her silver butterfly with trembly fingers. "I think we have an awkward customer. And the kettle, Hannah. I could murder a cuppa."

Elsie came over to Barbie. She looked at her hard and began to take off Barbie's clothes with spiny fingers.

"Shall I pour the milk, Mrs Treherne?" said Hannah.

"They can wait. Just set out the beakers. I'm about flaked out."

Elsie finished taking off Barbie's clothes then she led her to a child's chair. "Get up," Elsie said. Barbie could see Mrs Treherne looking at her.

"I am now going to attempt to drink this coffee," said Mrs Treherne in a high voice.

She backed onto her desk and sat an the edge still looking at Barbie. She motioned Elsie and Hannah to sit beside her. Then she lit a cigarette and gave one each to Elsie and Hannnah. Elsie looked across at

Barbie, her eyes flicked up to the ceiling and she sighed. Hannah was coughing on the cigarette.

"Too street-wise for me," Mrs Treherne said and blew a furry spout of smoke towards Barbie. "They drag them up and throw them to us like raw meat."

Elsie nodded sympathetically. "Were you once a teacher, Mrs Treherne?"

"Was I! Don't remind me. I can spot disruptives a mile off."

Hannah stubbed out her cigarette. "Shouldn't have liked to be in your class, Mrs Treherne," she said. Elsie looked at her sharply.

"It's a question of discipline," said Mrs Treherne. "That's why I left. We weren't allowed to use discipline." She gave a tap to her cigarette and the grey end fell off. Her other hand went to the bottom of a small boy who had crept towards them and she pushed him towards the sand tray.

"I'll mention discipline in your reports," said Mrs Treherne, "its importance and its function. Of course we're fighting the parents all the time." She stopped for a second then her lips pressed tighter. "It's the men I blame." She let her eyes float stonily round the painted figures on the walls. "You can't do anything without a positive man in the house."

She took a long suck at her cigarette then stubbed it quickly in a saucer. "You can give them the milk now," she said to Hannah. Elsie put out her cigarette and as Hannah poured out the milk, the room began to rattle with the children's cries.

"Queue!" shouted Mrs Treherne. She came over to Barbie "Right!" she said loudly. "I expect you're dry now. Put her things back on, Elsie, but give her the cloth first."

Elsie made circles with the cloth, pointing to the floor. Barbie got down and started mopping the floor and felt her damp pants clinging to her legs.

When she had finished Mrs Treherne's thick stockings appeared at the side of her head. "Come over here," she said. She took Barbie's shoulder with a hand like a hook and led her to the far wall which was painted a sky-blue colour. On the wall bobbed the yellow balloons on strings. Each balloon had a child's name in black felt-tip. Some of the balloons were higher than others. They rose up like fountains of golden bubbles near to where a polystyrene cloud hung near the ceiling. Mrs. Treherne took a new balloon from her pocket and blew it up. Then she wrote "Barbie" on it in black.

"Every time a child is good I move its balloon up in the sky. If it's bad I move it down again." She looked hard at Barbie. "Any child whose balloon touches the cloud gets a prize." She took from her pocket a packet of small iced biscuits and shook it in Barbie's face. Barbie's legs were beginning to smart.

"I'm starting your balloon halfway up. Try to get it to the top." She led Barbie over to the water tank and left her at the side of the small girl.

By the afternoon Barbie grew tired of the plastic ducks. She was taller than the other children and she leaned over the centre of the tank to where it sloped down in the middle. She fumbled for a few seconds in the deepest part and heard the water beginning to gurgle. The small girl laughed and the others watched as the water swirled and emptied down the pipe. Barbie looked up. Elsie and Hannah were talking quickly to Mrs Treherne at her desk.

Suddenly Mrs Treherne raised her arms and let them fall. "Well get her out, then!" She shouted. "She'll drive me starkers!"

Elsie rushed over to the water tank. She grabbed Barbie's hand and half-dragged her to a cupboard. As they flew past the wall the rush of air fanned the balloons which swooped as if they were trying to chase her. Before the cupboard door closed Barbie had just time to see Mrs Treherne's face like a fire and her fingers fluttering at her brooch.

Barbie could see the other children through the keyhole. They were lying down on carpet strips and some were already asleep. Crouched in the dust she nearly went to sleep herself when she heard Mrs Treherne say "Right! Everything away. It's a quarter to."

Barbie could hear doors opening and closing and Elsie and Hannah shouting. She was thinking about her balloon when a bright light exploded. Mrs Treherne stood there like a grey tree.

"Come out," she said, "we must have words." She took hold of the back of Barbie's neck. "However. all in good time. There's another thing to do."

She pulled Barbie out of the cupboard. Everybody had gone and the windows were black with early winter. Together they marched over to the sky-blue wall.

Mrs Treherne pointed to Barbies balloon. "That comes down in the morning if things don't improve." She bent down, placed her hands like knives under Barbie's armpits, and held her up. "If things don't improve- down it comes! Do-you-understand?" Her voice went as high as a scream and she gave Barbie a rattling shake like emptying a money-box.

Mrs Treherne put her down and began to draw all the curtains. Barbie went over to the water tank near the window and waited. She leaned on the glass edge and stared at the blue water which had almost stopped rocking.

Then MrsTreherne was suddenly beside her. The butterfly was quivering as if it was going to fly off Mrs Treherne's chest. She grabbed the child's chair which Barbie had stood on and placed it next to the water tank. Then she climbed on it to draw the curtains over the water tank.

Barbie suddenly felt a thud on her shoulder and there was a crash as Mrs Treherne fell almost on her head. The great splash nearly cleared the tank of its plastic ducks which leapt out, shedding great stars of wetness on the floor.

Mrs Treherne lay with her head just inside the tank. From the edge a red stain began to slide down the thick glass wall. As MrsTrehene lay inside the tank, water crept up her grey dress turning it black until it reached the butterfly. Her eyes were wide open and rolling and she was staring at a plastic duck which ebbed and flowed to her mouth as her breathe made little waves.

Barbie came closer and watched the water as it drowned the butterfly which sank and trapped some pearl bubbles beneath its wings. She looked, for the first time, into Mrs Treherne's eyes which strained like glass marbles. Barbie inspected every bit of her face. There was hardly any movement, and Mrs Treherne seemed to be smiling at last.

Barbie reached into the tank and took hold of Mrs.Treherne's hair so that her head and the butterfly were lifted out of the water. She felt the slow breath near her cheek. Then she let the head go and it splashed like a heavy ball. Mrs Treherne's mouth was in the water and bubbles started to burst from it. They began to build up like foam squeezed from a soap bottle. They spread over the surface until even the duck disappeared. Barbie watched the swelling bubbles for so long that she nearly went to sleep in the peaceful air of the playroom, until the knocking at the uncurtained window grew louder.

A familiar round face, clown-like in its peacock paint bobbed at the window frame. Its purple lips sprang apart. Its green-ringed eyes flicked round the playroom. In a few seconds they switched back to Barbie. Barbie laughed. Her mother's face was on the same level as the painted faces on the wall, as if one had come to life. Then Barbie felt cold. Her mother's face flashed punishment to come. Like a startled floppy puppet it was snatched from sight.

The bubble pile had stopped growing. Barbie carried the chair carefully to the sky-blue wall. Her balloon was only half way up so she could reach it easily. Her thick little nails slid round the drawing pin.

Before she pulled it out she looked back to where Mrs Treherne lay. Her dress was nearly black with the water and her legs were splayed more like a spider than a lady. Though her eyes were wide open Barbie knew she saw nothing. Before her mother opened the door she took the balloon and pinned it a little above the next highest on the wall.

Executive Toy

When anybody new sat in the Astra's passenger seat, the first thing they saw was Bob and his long funny legs dangling over the dashboard. They would smile. Most would laugh at his rubber orange body, his trembling eyes, and the little red tongue which waggled. Once one of Dennis's friends tried to steal Bob, but as he pulled his hand from his pocket Bob's long rubber legs flopped out and gave him away.

Dennis would say, "Oh that's Bob! You can't buy *him* in the shops, you know."

Then if they were still interested, Dennis would tell them how he was given Bob by the firm which employed him as a computer representative. Still interested (and Dennis could assess people with a salesman's eye) he would tell them how he put his entire trust in Bob. Actually Bob was a very expensive executive toy. You couldn't get him in the shops because he was part of the firm's sales pitch.

You could always tell about people like Dennis. He was one of the white nylon shirt brigade you see all the time in motorway cafes working out their expenses. The Astra was Dennis's travelling pad and, apart from the neatly pressed jacket swinging from the hanger at the back, Bob was its most valued occupant.

Bob was stuck to the inside of the windscreen on the left side and with every vibration of the car his eyes and his tongue would race round their plastic bubbles and come to rest. Each time with a different expression. Dennis could read these expressions which told him if success was waiting round the corner. Usually it applied to sales but once when Dennis tried to seduce a girl in the car Bob had altered his face when the car jiggled. The eyes and the mouth had formed a disapproving look. Dennis knew no good would come of his efforts. The girl called him a pervert when he stopped prematurely and re-hooked her bra. He mentioned the fact of Bob's expression and the girl grabbed the toy and crushed it in an angry fist. Bob rebounded in his infuriating way. The girl crushed it it an angry fist. Bob rebounded in his infuriating way. The girl flung insults at Bob, called Dennis a little boy and shouted that he really needed a rubber woman. Then she wrenched herself out of the car. As they sped off Bob was quickly restored to the windscreen, from where he grinned amiably back at the zooming shrinking figure of the girl.

It might have sounded silly, but events had proved that Bob was invariably right - or that Dennis's interpretation of his demeanour was correct. If Dennis was anxious about closing a sale he had simply to look at Bob's face when the car stopped outside the prospect's office. If Bob looked favourable, Dennis could enter the office with confidence. It always worked, though doubters might think that Dennis's increased faith was the major factor in the equation.

Not only was Bob a sort of talisman, he was a constant companion for Dennis. When Dennis was heartily sick of Radio 2, he would switch off and explain his fears and hopes for the future to Bob. Only yesterday Bob had got him out of a potentially nasty spot once when Dennis was hot on the trail of a particularly big order in London. He had been mobiled right up in Manchester. The roads in Lancashire were full of potholes and Bob's tongue wobbled dangerously. It wasn't much better when they got down Cheshire way. Bob's expression, anybody could tell, was thunderous, his eyes as cold as a witch's teat.

Dennis stopped at a roadside hotel and had a stiff Pimm's. He wished he could give one to Bob. When he came out, before he started the engine, he glanced at Bob perched in the windscreen. No change. Bob remained poker-faced. Dennis drove slowly through the Hampshire countryside. If he was late he might lose the sale. Was defying Bob worth it? He switched on the radio to take his mind off things and put his foot down. He was already half an hour late.

He was at Wimbledon when the news came through. An IRA bomb had blasted an office block. Incredibly it was the same in which the client lived. If he had been in time he might now be in little pieces distributed over Canary Wharf. He looked at Bob whose eyes swung merrily. The little red tongue had sunk down to a central position in his mouth, giving him a pouting self-satisfied look. Dennis silently kissed two fingers, reached across and pressed them against the little man's orange rubber bosom.

"When I've made my pile, Bob, I shan't forget you," Dennis spoke in snatches but quite loudly as the car purred along. If people saw him talking like this they might think he was mad, or singing with the radio. Well, let them. "I shan't forget you, even if I marry a beauty queen. When we get that big house. Get regraded to a Volvo. And that indexed pension. And that share option. And get a real leather briefcase instead of this tacky plastic one. Even if we have children. You won't be forgotten, old pal."

He turned slightly to smile at Bob. Bob smiled back. A heavy lorry rumbled close and Bob's eyes fluttered up in alarm. Dennis glanced sideways. "Bastard!" he shouted and let the lorry overtake.

He stopped in a layby to leaf through his forward orders. Now, with the falling through of the London job he had some time on his hands. There were some upgrade and add-ons orders to place. But there was one full system enquiry up in Yorkshire. It was worth closing fast as it might lead to a network order. He could get there before evening.

Lots of people have mascots and lucky charms. Rabbit foot. Copper bracelets. Lucky ducks. Joan the Wad. And that's just in the civilised countries. The old wisdoms of native and jungle haunts seem to help even backward people to survive. Of course a lot of people said it was just what Dennis read into Bob's changing rubber face. So it was really Dennis playing games with himself. Perhaps computer people get like that, staring at blank screens, solitary, hoping for messages out of the ether, lonely. Perhaps Dennis was like that after boring silent journeys like this one. When he suddenly met chattering clients and entered busy exploding offices filled with pretty secretaries it was like flowering lollipops beckoning him at the end of a long stalk.

As he travelled north the green budbursts in the hedgerows faded to bare branches. Quarries, cooling towers, deserted mineshafts and muddled allotments crowded by the road. Dennis put the heater on low and stared up at a wet flannel sky. The only bright thing in the car was Bob vibrating away on the shelf. Although the roads became twistier Dennis threw a glance or two at Bob. He was relieved to see Bob's eyes brighten, his little red tongue wiggling furiously. It was the portent of a good sale. Perhaps the beginning of a long stream of orders.

Dennis called the number on his mobile phone and heard a heavy Yorkshire accent reply. Dennis would have described the tone as dour. Then he remember that dourness was something the Scots claimed. A bit further North. Perhaps it was just the well-known brusqueness of Yorkshire folk. He mentioned a time for the meeting then rang off and gave his attention again to the winding road. Bob was still winking like a mad thing from the corner of the windscreen. There was no room for doubts in Bob's features. His face said it all. Go for it! It was a small enough firm. Blind them with computerspeak, emphasise the grave technicality of the system, then how easily it could be solved by an expert,minimum cost base, future downsizing of the labour force ...

He arrived in Leeds with time to spare. Parking was easier than in London, and no bombs to worry about here. As he locked the car door he could have sworn that Bob gave him a rubber thumbs-up signal.

The presentation was a disaster before it began. Worsnip, the company accountant, had it all laid out, ironed and filed away before he even started. The concentrated location of forward orders was too simple to require a computer. They had ample stocks of invoice and delivery forms for years to come and the staff had agreed, with union backing, to standstill wages for the next three years. Worsnip was your down-to-earth Yorkshireman, fair but blunt. Dennis's exuberance seeped out like unhealthy pus. The only thing Dennis left was his card, which Worsnip tore up before Dennis had closed the door.

It was beginning to rain. He opened the car door slowly, still feeling cold and sweaty from rejection. The first thing he saw was Bob who was hunched in the corner of the windscreen. The plastic casings shrouded his eyes and tongue were dull and dead-looking. Dennis scowled. Bob had given him every encouragement. He almost imagined that Bob was whimpering. He started the car, and immediately the soft purring engine shook Bob's eyes into a startled grin. Dennis had another customer in Carlisle and he might just make it over the Pennines. Bob was laughing now. Perhaps he had been off form? Perhaps it was all part of a plan, and an even bigger deal awaited him in the northwest?

The weather forecast told of a cold front, even snow on high ground. Dennis needed time to relax after the Leeds business and he decided not to go by the M62. Although the sky was darkening he felt as though he wanted to lose himself in winding roads over the hills rather than face civilisation just yet. He might put up at country pub.

It was six o'clock before he cleared the foothills. His anger had died away by now. He looked at Bob over in the corner. Bob seemed unnaturally subdued.

"All right," Dennis said, as if to reconcile him. "Do we go on or stop for a cuddle?"

As he was looking at Bob a powerful car cruised past. He swerved and had just time to see it was a hearse which contained four men coming back from a job still in their black crepe garb and top hats. They seemed to be on their way back from a funeral and were convulsed with laughter at some joke.

When Dennis looked at Bob he was vibrating uncontrollably, laughing and eager.

"Right," said Dennis, "Carlisle it is!"

A sudden shower of snow crystals hit the windscreen and Dennis put the wipers on. Outside the car, telegraph poles flew past leaping alongside like mad things over hedges and side roads. The car took the smaller hills like a powerful wave. Then it began to stutter at the crest of each rise. It could have been the cold air blasting in at the radiator and freezing the water inlet pipe.

Dennis looked at Bob. The whitened road ahead showed that he was the only traveller about. Bob's eyes danced merrily.

Dennis knew it must be the electrics when the dashboard lights went out. There was nothing but the gleeful eyes of Bob catching the white light that poured into the car. It was then that Dennis knew that Bob had let him down again. He had an empty feeling that Bob's luck and his own had run out. That this was, quite literally, the end of the road. He reached down and put the handbrake on. Then he leaned across and took Bob's legs, opened the window, and threw Bob as far as he could into a bank of ling.

He pulled at the inside bonnet catch and got out of the car. The feathery touch of large snowflakes brushed at his cheek. When he opened the bonnet and flashed his torch he could just see burn marks and a bare trailing lead. It was a short-out after all. If he could insulate the lead he could light a cigarette, wait a few minutes, and the battery would recover. There was nothing suitable to tie off the lead. Then he thought of Bob. He plunged into the heather at the side of the road and felt wet tufts spring up his calves. He cast about for a minute in the increasing whiteness with his torch. Then by the sheerest luck he spotted Bob's long legs nearly covered and lifted them to his mouth and kissed them in a theatrical gesture. Bob's eyes pointed like demon sparks as he carried him back to the car.

The rubber legs were quickly tied in place. Bob's eyes looked surprised, almost in pain. And in spite of himself Dennis couldn't keep back a grin at the orange legs twisted in the life-saving knot. Bob looked for all the world as if he keenly wanted to go to the lavatory.

At that moment Dennis felt the car move. It slid back and he rushed along it to open the door. It came up against a roadside rock and mercifully ground to a halt after a few feet. He quickly reached inside and pulled the handbrake harder. When he closed the door he noticed the flood of warm oil melting the snow at his feet. He climbed into the car and closed the door. It was fairly obvious that the sump had cracked on the boulder. He lit a cigarette and as the snow blotted out the windows, he thought of Bob's strangled limbs under the bonnet.

After they removed Dennis's frozen body and dusted the car to eliminate the possibility of foul play, the police opened the bonnet and found Bob perched above the battery. His legs and arms were wound in a crazy knot round his groin. The plastic bubbles encasing his eyes were iced up, and his blank expression stared out wistfully at the folly of this world.

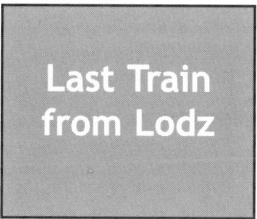

Last Train from Lodz

I keep the photograph of my wife on the table where I can see it. The mantlepiece is too far for my old eyes.

Beside it is a picture of Charles. I received a letter today from him telling me that I am a "great-grandfather". My wife would have been ecstatic had she lived. I used to tell her about those early days.

Dark fog. The spit of steam. Shrieking whistles. Carriage doors crashing like cannon. 1939, just before the war, and I had completed an export deal in Lodz. The train creaked and jostled its way, pushing sweeping curtains of darkness and wetness aside, as we shambled towards the Polish frontier. It was all quite silly. There was no hope of the order ever being delivered. The textile samples I carried in my attache case meant nothing. In days, perhaps hours, we would be at war. This was the last train out.

I tried the couchette several times but the clanking of points and the bellowing of the guards made sleep a kind of torture. I had a bottle, but the occupants of my carriage made it difficult to indulge. They were a young couple hardly in their thirties and the most adorable child you ever set eyes on.

I should describe my appearance, without sounding too vain. I have - sorry - had a mop of fair hair and I am fairly tall. This had a different effect on different Europeans. The Germans looked on me as a fellow Aryan, and they respect height. Other nationalities took me for a dozy Swede (except the Swedes) and thought me an easy touch with an exploitable level of angst. I was, and still am, an ordinary grammar school product from Birmingham.

When we reached the German border I bought a copy of the *Allgemeine Zeitung*. It had the usual rantings and ravings, anti-semitic threats, preparing its readers for the coming abominations. Aristotle, we were taught, said "Man is by nature a political animal." I had seen enough of the Nazis to know that they were highly political as well as animals. My friends at home would not believe my stories about them. The day must come when they would destroy themselves and I often longed to have a part in their downfall.

The couple opposite me were unusually quiet and the child was extremely well behaved. The picture of them sitting opposite aroused all the old feelings of the childlessness of my own marriage. Our hopelessness in the face of Nature's perversity. If only God could have blessed us with a similar angel!

I could see that the family were Jews. The olive skins of the parents, their features, and their dark hair marked them unmistakably. The beauty of their child had that ethereal touch which many Jewish children carry until their teens. The boy had luxuriant locks and a rich garland of curls. A bewitching god of a child.

Each time we came to a station, or if the train shuddered to a halt in the flat expanse of the northern plain, fear would sit on the faces of the parents. The woman asked if she could have the carriage lights dimmed. I consented readily thinking she wished to sleep. It became obvious that fear hovered outside, on the platforms, and in the guttural challenges of the troops who patrolled the line.

The man clutched a brief case. Sometimes he opened it nervously to pull out a slice of wurst and bread. After an interval I spoke to them in German knowing that most Poles had a knowledge of the language.

"Do you travel far, *mein herr?*"

The man seemed uncertain of his reply.

The woman said, "We go to the coast. To Nederlands."

The man looked sharply at her as if she had betrayed a secret.

I said jocularly, "Then we shall be together for a long time. I am English and am going home."

This seemed to cheer them up. The man offered blutwurst. "I took you for a Skandinavisch," he said.

"Many people do."

He wasted no time in introducing his child, Karl, who bowed from the waist and clicked his heels gravely. Somehow I could imagine him on a concert platform in full evening dress receiving the plaudits of a crowd. He seemed to be extremely well-fed, in fact stouter than was strictly healthy. He offered me a bag of boiled sweets, which is as far as a little boy's friendship can press on a first acquaintance.

My presence seemed to give them repose, but their anxiety became noticeable when we stopped again. By this time I had and persuaded Karl to sit on my knee. He produced, and I read him, *Schnee*

Weiss und der Sieben Zwergen. Karl had kindly but firmly refused to read it himself but was vastly amused by my terrible German accent.

When we reached the German border the train slowed. The man looked anxiously out of the window. I could hear the demands for *"Papieren, bitte!"* echoing up and down in the greasy air outside. People got on and off. The chill acid light of the station plated the wet platform. The iron casque of one of Hitler's troopers loomed up against the window. There was shouting. Then silence.

I looked across at the young couple. The man had his fingers wrapped round his wife's wrist and he was gripping so tightly that her flesh blenched from the force of his grasp.

In a minute he got up and peered out into the corridor. His wife remained seated but she drew the little boy in front of her. She stared manically into his eyes as if trying to convey a message by the scorching focus of her gaze. Then her eyes roamed over his face as if to imprint his features on her mind. She spoke to him rapidly in a low voice and my German comprehension gave out.

The husband opened the carriage door. The train had started again and was picking up speed. He beckoned his wife. They stood at the open door whispering, their heads bent together. The man pointed to his briefcase which lay on the seat he had just vacated. Karl seemed quite unconcerned at the tension.

Then the train suddenly stopped. I had heard the Wehrmacht shouting before. But this was the harsher voice of Waffen SS. It seemed to start way down the line and grow louder. Then it too stopped. People boarded the train and it began to move very quickly. The couple at the carriage door seemed to have made their mind up about something. Their features blazed with a sudden light. They looked at Karl, then at me. Then they were gone. I heard their footsteps hurrying, running, down the corridor as if they were trying to put as much space as possible between us and themselves.

My mind fought for control of the situation. I didn't really understand what was happening until I heard a shot and a scream and more shouting. Then I knew what I had to do.

I closed the sliding door and opened the window wide. The black wind tore like a scouring knife at the air inside the carriage. Karl stood silently as I cut off his hair with the tailor's scissors from my sample case. He remained perfectly still. His dark locks flew into the fog and were lost down the track. Then I took off most of his clothes and threw some out of the window as well. I kept a few and stuffed them into my attache case.

When I had pared him down to one set of clothes he looked almost as thin as most of the new class of refugees who had begun to wander round Europe. He kept very still as I made my preparations, and I had the impression I was dealing with a beautiful compliant doll.

The train was going well now, a rhythmic clicking of the rails almost proclaiming that we were now out of yokel Poland and into the efficiently oiled Third Reich. I took out the wurst and bread and dumped them on the seat. There were only the wads of banknotes left. I threw them in the briefcase and into the roaring night and closed the window.

There was still no sound from the corridor. I wrenched both sliding doors fully open for anyone to walk in. Then I took Karl on my knee. I began patiently: "My name is Charles. I am English. This is my father. *Konnten Sie das bitte wiederholen?*" He repeated it quite well, and nearly perfectly after a few times.

I gave him a slice of sausage. I spoke very correct if wobbly German. "Now, please. We play a game. *Sprech spielen? Ja?*" He nodded. "*Sprechen sie in Englisch*"

Karl smiled. He peered at the page and, stuttering to cue, he pressed out the English words in painful syllables. He smiled impishly. I gripped his little shoulder and repeated and gabbled the words in a kind of desperation. He looked up in fright. Then he repeated the English words without taking his eyes off me. I whispered a few more instructions to him.

By the time the figure appeared at the door I looked up as languidly as I could as the trooper shouted *"Papieren!"* Then I stood up slowly, unrolling myself to my full height. I could see that his glance flickered appreciatively to my blond top. I handed him my passport stuff. He studied it.

"*Englische - Vertreter? Textile?*" He tried to sound important.

"Yes, old man, commercial traveller," I said, knowing that he barely understood me.

"*Kind? Papieren, bitte?*" He pointed to Karl.

"Charles?" I said to Karl. "Say your name."

Karl stood up with the book in his hand whilst I fumbled about in my attache case tossing out the children's clothes as if searching.

He looked quite vulnerable with his shorn locks. "My name is Charles," he said. "I am English." He began reading loudly the first sentence in English, "Once upon a time there was a young girl called Snow White." Then he stopped.

A thin face appeared behind the trooper. He had the soft hat of an officer. He studied the scene for a moment.

"*Ist genug!*" he barked. The soldier ducked out. The officer slammed the doors and they moved to the next compartment. The two of us reached Amsterdam on September 1st.

Charles is now in his late fifties. I tried to get him interested in the textile business but quickly gave up when I remembered he had other gifts. He intends to give his farewell performance on the London stage next year. No strutting politician, no fatuous telly personality is safe from his searing wit as he mimics their mannerisms and turns of speech to perfection.

His letter goes on to say that he and his wife will be making their annual visit quite soon. I shall meet them at the station as always. Charles loves railway stations. They are, as he says, for remembering those to whom you never wish to say goodbye.

Long Blond Hair

After all these years I have to tell my typewriter about Miss Youhill.

Miss Youhill came to us in the middle of a term.

"I hope that you will be kind to Miss Youhill who has joined us for a few weeks."

It was a silly thing for Miss Renton to say. We all knew that Miss Youhill was a student teacher. And that was the next best thing to a holiday for us.

When Miss Renton left the room with a great beam of relief some of the others at the back started to play her up without waiting. Miss Youhill had fair hair and a string of coffee coloured beans which shone like chocolate so that you wanted to bite them. She had no idea of getting out the things for handicraft and tried to get Blackie and his gang to help.

That was a mistake and we finished up being ready just as the bell went. She never raised her voice and she peered at Blackie running and shouting round the desks as if she didn't believe it. We knew she was the kind of teacher who wouldn't raise her voice let alone her hand. She was very pretty. Long blond hair.

At first I nearly died laughing at Blackie's antics, and when Miss Renton slipped in one day she thought Miss Youhill had made us laugh with some joke and she quickly went out smiling to herself. After I saw Miss Youhill dabbing her eyes on the way to the staff room I tried to be kind to her, and I saw to it that the smaller boys didn't laugh when Blackie started up again.

Blackie twisted my arm in the playground when he saw I wasn't joining in. He gave me a Chinese burn and did another thing which I won't bother mentioning.

Mr Fawcett came in about a week after she started. He may have come to help too because Miss Youhill looked a lot older and her

The Singing Men

eyes were redder and she sometimes turned to the blackboard and stood there, trembling with her back towards us. Mr Fawcett was head of handicraft and had a fat wife and several fat children. He had black hair like a Phillips stick-on sole and he looked pale like Miss Youhill but he was strong, and he stared Blackie down and whispered to him at the back of the class. I heard the end of it. It sounded like "...your bleeding face." But Blackie said he was only asking about homework.

On Wednesday games afternoon Miss Youhill took the girls for Lacrosse, and Mr Fawcett refereed the football. Blackie and his gang were on the other side and when Mr Fawcett wasn't looking, gave all our forward line the "dead leg" after asking us which leg we kicked with. It was almost impossible to kick the ball after that and they won, fourteen - nil.

I didn't go back to the changing room because Mr Fawcett told us to get on with it and he went across to the next field for a word with Miss Youhill. I knew that Blackie was waiting for our team in the shower so I thought I'd just go straight home and get washed there.

It was getting misty near four o'clock and I took the short cut by the reed beds, over the stinking beck where we sometimes got newts. It was then I saw Mr Fawcett and Miss Youhill near some trees. They were talking and didn't notice me and after a bit Mr Fawcett put his arm round her. I was very surprised and I got a queer lump which kept jumping in my throat and making breathing difficult. But it had gone by the time I sat down for tea, though I didn't want any tea.

I nearly told Blackie the next day. He might have let me join the gang. But he got me in an arm-lock before assembly so I didn't tell him and I didn't tell anybody else.

"She'll not last a fortnight," Blackie said. He was standing on a seat in the lavvy one break-time. "I'm taking bets. You all have to have a bet, one way or the other," and he dropped his ciggy down with a hiss and blew the smoke straight at the smaller ones.

When I went home I went the way to see if any newts had spawned yet. I wasn't hiding in the reeds but I knew they hadn't seen me, because he was holding her again, this time with both hands, and she was shaking her head. I thought that it was about time Mr Fawcett got home to his own wife and children who were probably screaming their heads off, instead of patting a teacher he had hardly known for two weeks.

I think the newts were just on the point of having babies and I took care to go that way home every evening. Near the end of the week they were there again . And this time he kissed her, on the forehead, like my mother did when I went to school camp. Then I saw Miss Youhill break away from him and stand a short distance away with her arms folded as if she was shivering. Fawcett came and put both arms around her shoulders. I nearly stepped out of the reeds to let him know that it was a public place. But she was shaking her head. She was probably telling him that his wife had his tea on the table.

We didn't see Miss Youhill after that. Miss Renton came back all smiling and gave Blackie the slipper just after prayers. Mum wanted to know if I'd been eating sweets, and why her steak pie wasn't good enough any more. Mr Fawcett looked paler than ever, and he kept Blackie in one night after school.

Blackie's a lot better now. He's stopped tweaking ears and he doesn't even talk to the rest of the class. But he was right about Miss Youhill. She didn't last a fortnight and she never came back. I told Mum I didn't eat sweets. She said I looked pale and ought to see the doctor. She thinks she's an absolute marvel with steak pie.

Lucinda Says

So far I've managed to keep myself to myself. All right, 'pure' if you want it in a word.

Oh I've seen the adverts in the papers. 'Sexy challenge from London publisher.' "What I want," says Tarquin Thrashbrush, "is women who can big write racy novels!"

I know what he wants. Big racy women who are into sex. Well, I've tried to avoid that sort of thing. Train fare down to London. Dinner at a big hotel, drunk on Soave and publishing chat. Then back to his place before he packs the damaged goods on the last milk train back up North.

Lucinda, my editor, has a pretty shrewd idea of men. They're all after one thing, Edith, she says. A pity. All we women in publishing can do is to try to turn the brute instinct into an Art Form. And, of course, make them pay for it. After her last depressing experience with the opposite sex she was more bitter than ever. "Dirty devil!" she exclaimed. "From now on I'm going to concentrate on my Work. Publishing is my life."

Lucinda has helped me a great deal in my writing. She was the one who taught me that the key to a story line is character. Think character, Lucinda says. Plotting will take care of itself. It grows from character. She gets very excited about that. And different locations throws character into high relief, she commands. We've had El Sherif and his mystic desert tents. You've given us Igor, cruel but fascinating in his snow-bound dascha. Now give us something new, Edith. And don't forget Steam Readership demands Steam! She means what we used to call "raunchy" passages. Well, I'm setting the next one in a banana plantation in Madeira. That should grab them, as they say.

Another thing, says Lucinda, you're supposed to visit the places you write about. Soak up the ambience, Edith, she cries. I tell her how can I on my pension? I suppose I could send away for some free brochures. Saga has some lovely cut-price holidays. Even cheaper in the off season.

Eleven books in print, and some down for repeats. Besides, Lucinda says, Eastern Europe shouldn't be forgotten. I think we've got Bulgaria interested.

But it's this "steam" thing that worries me. In today's world, says Lucinda, you can't shut the bedroom door on the reader. Times when the vision of a chaste ankle, or the scorch of a burning kiss, were enough to see us through the night are long since past. And what sort of kick can you get from a row of asterisks? Readership demands Steam! Not, of course, for Steam's sake. We can leave that to the telly. But honest, physical Steam crammed with tender meaningful insights.

Why can't we put that sort of thing on the cover? I ask. Back comes the answer: Readership won't wear it. And there are reasons. It is not House Policy to compete with the vulgar type of bodice-ripper, Lucinda says. It is not our market profile. Text and cover are different product symbols. We are talking premier quality writing, Edith. We do not purvey titillation.

So there you are. I don't know if I can do it, I tell her. It's over forty years since I lost Alfred and you forget things.

I've been with Lucinda for seven years, ever since she left Oxford. Came down, I think they call it. I haven't been writing much longer. Lucinda brought me this far and I hate to disappoint her. Seven years, she said, is a long time in this business to stick with one House, Edith. But I'm the loyal type. Loyal to our readers, and loyal to you. Most of my ladies are mature persons, like you, in the meridian of their lives. (I liked that: "In the meridian of their lives." But I don't think I could use it for my kind of reader.)

You have a flair for romantics, she says. She wouldn't think of putting me on historicals or regional sagas. There's life in the old dog yet! as she phrases it. I respect you, Edith, she says. You are one of the doers of this world. It's all right for people like me, sitting in the office, doing my nails and swearing at the tea girl. But I couldn't write like you. Oh yes, I can excercise my critical faculties, identify current market trends, calculate break-even print runs, evaluate marginal product costs. But I couldn't make it happen like you, Edith.

Of course, I never actually met Lucinda. I've told her - I sometimes think of you, Lucinda, down in London. Wine bars, Stringfellows, dancing the night away. It must be exciting to be young and have a job like that!

Don't even think about it! she says. It's sheer Hades! A fortune on clothes. Impossible to avoid the saturated fats. We're talking cellulite, Edith! And perhaps you've heard about the price of studio flatlets? Consider yourself lucky, my girl, she says. Think of the charge you get when you see another of your 'babies' in print for the first time, waggling its tiny paragraphs! But seriously, I could never get that charge, Edith. So I thought, give me good old Leeds, I suppose, everytime.

Just before *Dusky Savage* came out (the one that started me off) Lucinda invited me for tea at the Dorcester. Something went wrong with the trains at Wolverhampton, and I never got as far as King's Cross. I didn't try it again. But Lucinda always sends me House Newsletters, Market Reports, and especially Reader's Letters and Queries. Reader Feedback she calls it.

Sometimes the postman tries to stuff a sackful in the letter box and he has to ring the bell, and I have to come down in my dressing-gown and curlers. I have this wire basket, you see, under the letterflap. I don't like things falling on the doormat where people wipe their feet, and then putting the post straight on the breakfast table. It's one of my pet niggles.

Lucinda is very fair. She sends the favourable letters and the "awkward" ones. Except of course, those from certian very sick men. Some readers want the price of books to be reduced. Sometimes readers want bigger print or more pages. (House Rules are very strict about the number of pages. Ignore those at your peril! Edith, Lucinda says. They are beyond the parameters of viable production. Which means you can't do it.) Sometimes they want to change the heroine's clothes and jewellry, and I have to go out and buy the latest fashion magazines. Put it on expenses for the tax man, Lucinda says. Sometimes they even want the colour of her eyes changed. I mean, I've been through twinkling hellebore green, impish cornflour blue and throbbing mulberry purple. What do they want? You can't have a heroine with red eyes. Use the thesaurus, Lucinda says. If flowers have worked for you, start on precious stones, painters' pigments - anything! Leave flowers, she says, if you've done flowers.

Readership, says Lucinda, demands high sophisticated standards. Readership is constantly evolving. You can't argue with evolution. Most of the letters are downright soft. But some are really abusive. Some of them make me wish I'd never got into the business, but I'm used to it, and I've bought this word processor...

There was one woman - called herself 'nauseated' of Wolverhampton (where I missed my train, remember?). She wrote to say that my *Blossoms in the Dust* had successfully corrupted her teenage daughter. Called me an "unprincipled young harridan". That made it all seem worthwhile, somehow! In *Blossoms,* on Lucinda's suggestion, I had boldly stepped through the bedroom door and given it plenty of Steam.

'Nauseated' had obligingly enclosed with her letter the offending pages 135 and 136. (I always aim for some kind of crisis three quarters of the way through, by the way - Lucinda's tip.) On the bottom of this letter Lucinda had written in red biro "take no notice. Silly frustrated woman! You are doing a great job!"

I wrote back, nevertheless, to 'Nauseated' (without, of course, supplying my name and address - House Rules again!) pointing out that she was the only one who had ever complained about my language, and that one must keep up with evolving standards.

As it happened, in the same post, I had this letter from 'Mere Male' of Solihull, stating just the opposite point of view. It was refreshing to have a masculine point of view. (Lucinda says that market research proves that ninety-eight per cent of readers are overwhelmingly female.)

After praising plot and character construction, 'Mere Male' went on to say that he was an avid reader of this genre of fiction, and that he had followed my output with great interest since I started. He could trace my development from *Dusky Savage* right through to *Illicit Harvest*. The young man (I imagine he was young by the sensitive tone of his letter) said that my writing style now revealed a mature virility it had hitherto lacked. In my progress from novice wordsmith to professional stylist I had at last found my "voice". And this no doubt converged with my growth from fragile girlhood to ripening womanhood. Would I go further, as I had done so much to expose gender hypocrisy and tear away the final vestiges of reserve? Call a spade a spade, and have done with tip-toeing away at the crucial moment of consummation?

I didn't give him my real name and address, though he begged for both. Lucinda had forgotten to add any of her perceptive barbs to that particular letter. I toyed with the idea of pretending to ask her opinion, but instead I decided to pen a reply.

I simply wrote briefly to 'Nauseated' of Wolverhampton stating that I regretted her carping approach but I was confident she didn't represent Enlightened Readership, even in the Midlands. I went on to suggest that she might care to see a more typical letter of constructive criticism. And I sent her the letter from "Mere Male".

I realise now that this was wrong. All reader's replies should go through Lucinda - House Rules - but I couldn't restrain myself. (Am I getting more emotional with age?)

I wrote back to "Mere Male" saying that his impetuous high spirits must surely be a product of his youth, and that the typical readership bracket rested on a more mature feminine response. I was not - repeat not - seeking to "turn anyone on" (to use his own phrase). Rather to entertain without offending. To reveal relationships rather than to instruct in the mechanics of love-making.

You can see I intended it to be a fairly arms-length kind of reply.

A fortnight later Lucinda wrote back, using her famed red biro. We have a problem, she said, and it won't go away. We must either move it to the back burner, or take it on board. In my innocent eagerness I had "dropped her in it". She didn't invent House Rules - but my action had been highly inflamatory to Readership.

Rather a tart reply, I thought. But that was nothing to the bombshell which burst into the wire cage under my letterbox the next day. It seems I had forgotten, in my effort to bring together two different kinds of readership, to clip off the addresses on their respective letters!

Apparently, the daughter of 'Nauseated' had got hold of his letter and had written to 'Mere Male', apologising for her Mother's behaviour. A reply was sent, and before long an affectionate exchange of messages had taken place between the two young people. Romance had blossomed and had progressed much faster than any literary effort of mine could have prompted. "Nauseated" was suing for alienation of filial affections, citing the House as accessory before the fact.

Everything eventually turnd out for the best. 'Nauseated' was laughed out of court, and Lucinda said that the whole thing had brought much needed publicity to the House in the middle of what she called a non-positive sales trough. There would be a special Christmas gratuity in the post from the House to add to the Government's bonus for pensioners.

Lucinda made it clear, however, that we were not in "that kind of game" and that the Front Office had insisted that I change my pseudonym forthwith. I could barely stifle my excitement at having brought two people who were never, geographically, far apart. I understand, from what Lucinda says, that Jennifer and Lawrence have recently put down a deposit on a crofter's cottage deep in the Scottish Highlands.

Through Lucinda, they sent me a Christmas card last year and asked for a family snap in return. I sent them a photo of Alfred and myself taken during the war.

They say that fiction is life with the dull bits cut out. I tore the bottom off the photo so that Alfred's RAF uniform wouldn't show. (Thank goodness he wasn't wearing his forage cap!) Just his cheeky face and wavy brylcreemed hair. When I rubbed out *Cleethorpes 1943* from the back it looked as if it might have been taken yesterday.

    I sometimes wonder what would have happened if Alfred had come back from Berlin that night. He was the quiet type. Smoked a pipe and liked *ITMA*. We would have gone to Cleethorpes every year, where he had family. I might never have written these books...

Pig

I don't know who to blame it on. But I cannot think of Mrs Keogh without loathing. As a teacher I pride myself on an orderly logical mind. How else can I trust myself to communicate? If only they had left us alone!

Lucy is dead and beyond recall. And who, in a frenzy of distrust, called the police and put me in this place? Mrs Keogh.

Mrs Keogh simply accused the first person to hand. The one on whom she had lavished her hate these past seven years. The one who tried to bring her daughter all the happiness she ever craved. Who said that women always pay in the end?

I shall - in the circumstances - undoubtedly hang. Because all the evidence is - circumstantial.

Something changes when you get married. Nature takes over. There's really no other reason for getting married.

It was a perpetual disappointment to me as well as Lucy that we never had a baby. And we didn't need Mrs Keogh whispering in our ears every time Lucy looked seedy. We wanted to conform. How else could the commercial blandishments of *Mothercare* and the *Early Learning Centre* bring a lump to our throats.? Did we enjoy stepping off pavements to avoid wide twin-laden babybuggys?

These were lessons enough.

Sometimes I think Mrs Keogh wanted to creep into bed with us and supervise proceedings. As I said to Lucy, if she wanted to raise the statistical probability of having grandchildren she should have bestowed the miracle of birth on more numerous progeny. As it was she propelled Mr Keogh into an early grave, and Lucy was their only child.

I had, of course, done my best. My sperm tests had all been positive in respect of normality, viability, motility and all other testable desiderata.

Procreation came to dominate our lives. I never realized that nature could tyrannize to such an extent over liberated and intelligent-people. Our resolve to have children apparently placed us on the same level as peasants. Even they could give birth in fields on the way home from work and think nothing of it.

Never in my wildest pornographic dreams did I encounter ovulation charts. When I told Doctor Beesley that my main teaching subject was statistics, he immediately suggested that I kept graphical records of the peaks and troughs of Lucy's temperature. I stuck gold hopeful stars on those long swinging curves to indicate the dates of our "attempts".

After several months the *Habitat* wallpaper of our bedroom took on the appearance of a continuous panorama of decorated Christmas trees. It seemed to amuse Lucy that I used good conduct stars. Those were the early smiling days. I felt she was patting my head for performance and prowess.

Later, in the days of hollow eyes and accelerating headaches, I took sordid clinical tests with smirky young nurses handing me the bottle. Where had all the orange blossom gone?

Mrs Keogh's initial transparent simperings turned to ugly frowns. Her face wore the metallic sheen of the grotesque earrings and bangles she affected. Lips were pulled tight on sinews like dolly-bag drawstrings. More pointed allusions, in the face of all the medical evidence, were made concerning my virility. I was even tempted to show her my charts. Such was the depth of my humiliation.

The decision to buy a pig farm, like most of the later decisions, was made for a number of reasons. We had begun to distrust each other. We couldn't make incisive forays into the future. We temporized. We weighed the advantages. It is called planning. It is unnatural. It was as if we were pleading our cases before some weighty tribunal.

Pigs, we were told, meant profitable investment, provided they didn't succumb to swine fever. But there were other philoprogenic reasons. I firmly believe that we thought that pigs would change our natures.

That wasn't actually stated as a reason for going into the pig business. Our debut was a compound of cold business calculation and wild fantasy.

First, we needed a new joint interest which would absorb our energies and would help us to take a stand against the world. Selling pine furniture, or even health foods, hadn't the appeal of actual production. Secondly, I needed a new dimension and to give up my dyspeptic job in a worryingly inferior public school. I needed to make contact with reality.

Thirdly, (this ticking off of items is a dead giveaway for deeply unstated motivation!) Lucy needed somewhere to relax. In the nineteenth century lunatics were immured in rural locations in the hope that quiet earth rhythms would calm fevered minds. Stress, said Dr Beesley, was often a principal cause of non-fertilisation. Not only is an unfamiliar activity itself relaxing, but pig breeding would remove our initial anxieties to prove our fecundity, if we were succesful.

I know that this isn't entirely convincing. Imitation birth has a long history in fertility ritual. Pigs are nearest (monkeys apart) to our human condition. I can only say that few human activities are prompted by a clinical assesment of the cost/benefit type. Please God it may long be so.

Many other reasons, all half-formed were killing our environment. The farmers who would concrete over their green fields in search of another penny per acre would be taught a lesson by our methods. Animal rights would flourish. City life had failed. It needed aware spirits like ourselves to head-up the backlash.

The economics confirmed, if anything, these unquantifiable principles. I must say that, once the decision was taken, we threw ourselves into it body, soul and bank deposits. All in all we had enough to raise the ante for a sizable investment. No early financial struggles. We started from a viable capital base. I had a small lump sum from my few years of reckonable service in teaching.

The big surprise was Mrs Keogh. She chipped in handsomely, drawing much fatalistic comfort from the fact that she "wouldn't be here much longer and you can't spend it where I'm going." Although this left her destination indeterminate I could appreciate the general prospect. She didn't demand to come and live with us. Instead, she announced, in tremendously reasonable tones, that she would buy a Mini, learn to drive and visit us from time to time.

Porker's Drift was a near-level, well-grassed plot of about five hectares. We began in fine style with about one hundred sows.

Pigs are strong in the shoulder and have a deeply ingrained propensity to escape. Naturally, preliminary work involved the erection of strong fences. Next, as this part of the country is cool and cloud-blown, we built fully insulated huts. There are less expensive ways to house pigs but not with our principles. Also I felt that Mrs Keogh would have wished her capital to be devoted to this caring aspect of upkeep.

It was hard work. Harder than teaching in a public school. In some ways comparable, but richer, immensly richer, in purpose. Early mornings were spent dishing out our swill in ringing clean mists. We were out long before the city types had even dreamt of reaching for their umbrellas.

Perhaps I am making this sound over romantic, but, believe me, it was carried on against a background of hard won technical expertise. Pigs are greedy and wasteful - almost humanoid in an abandoned sort of way. As with our own diet, Lucy and I had to experiment with their food mix. If one is going for growth in pigs the rule is low fibre/high protein. This was at odds with our wholefood regime, yet understandable in porcine terms.

Mrs Keogh's first visit to our new location in her brand new Mini coincided with the boiling up of vegetable scraps and fish waste. Her expression of distaste amused us. Her disgust was somewhat mollified when she discovered that this onerous task fell, according to our agreed division of labour, more or less permanently to me. It was clear even at this stage that winning her support was going to be a drawn-out excercise. She was still critical of how her capital was being spent. I suppose I fell over myself in pointing out, in a nervous conversational way, the virtues of Large Whites and Saddlebacks.

I know now I over-stressed the returns we expected by breeding. All my talk of artificial insemination and second generation hybrid gilts would hardly be received with unfeigned rapture by a person of her sensitivity. She showed more interest in the later stages of the food chain. My ceaseless chatter concerning the curing of bacon, the production of sausages and generally processing pork (all, looking back, quite wild schemes of diversification) seemed to strike a more comfortable note.

And Lucy - I'd never seen her so happy! It was all worth it, just for that. We enjoyed the pride of independence and proprietorship. I firmly believe that everyone in this country should own a field. Even if it involves enforced deportation for some.

Earlier in our marriage I had attempted, often under cover of some thinly disguised therapy publication, to interest Lucy in sexual acrobatics early in the mornings. The only response was an anthem of low discouraging moans.

It was quite amusing how this pattern had changed. Now she was up, so to speak, with the pigs, talking excitedly of Florence and Hannah (why did she choose Victorian names?) or whichever of her sows was about to drop a litter that day. Yet our relations with each other were never better. Pigs did not so much dominate our lives as we entered into theirs. We would hold "pig conversations" over a bottle of wine in the evenings. Our tenderest contacts by mouth or touch would be accompanied by pig noises. Our love making would rehearse the intimate inspections we reserved for our charges. The darker side of our pig-talk contained references to anthrax, necrotic enteritis and other monsters of dread whose names we could hardly bring ourselves to repeat.

Whatever I may say later I must praise Lucy's dedication to our joint enterprise. I could describe her approach in no better terms than "maternal". Lucy's standards of husbandry and stockpersonship were exemplary. She could not abide antibiotics or growth promoters. Her ministrations were such that it was as if she found in pigs the living fulfilment of the children we could not have. Of course, when I say pigs, I mean sows. All males, except the odd breeding boar, were slaughtered within six months of birth. It is a woman's world in Pigland.

It was at this stage that I first noticed an antipathy between herself and her porcine charges. On reflection, it seems now amply obvious that the sows would resent the removal of the boar. And the added pique of being artificially and repeatedly fertilized by a female of a different species. This makes the final horrific tragedy easier to understand.

Lucy had always taken a strong positive role in our household. I have always taken a back but useful seat. Pig swill must be boiled for at least an hour; I boiled it. Quarters must be cleaned out each morning, especially at farrowing time; I was on hand with hot soapy water. Pigs must be weighed weekly; I was ready with notepad. They are, if anything, more trouble than humans. They tend to keel over if anything - ventilation, water, warmth, is amiss. They say a curly tensed tail is a very good indicator of a healthy pig. My cardinal role was to see that tails kept curly and tense at all times.

So what were Lucy's tasks? At first we had our supplies of semen delivered by rail and post and the local vet did the job of artificial insemination. That didn't last long. Lucy was prompted by some kind of longing for personal involvement in this final act of her relationship with pigs. She was very observant of the vet's professional manipulation of catheters and plastic bottles. She made herself an expert by imitation.

In her down-to-earth way she gave the vet his marching orders on that side of the business. I noted her concentration and the delightful quivering of her lower lip as she wandered about the herd checking which sows were on heat. Her cheeks shone with an almost religious light as she bent to assist Nature's work - I might say to the consternation of our furious boar, a beast we very soon got rid of as Lucy's efforts produced success.

I assisted in any way I could, boiling catheters, filling semen containers. But I must say that Lucy never let an opportunity pass or a receptive sow be spared a pregnancy. Our bank balance and the state of our cash flow were worldly testimony to her efforts. Though these were asides to her fierce dedication and the satisfaction she reaped from her genitive task. Of course she excused her role as Fertilisation Queen by saying that it saved the cost of the vet and the boar and reduced the chances of transmitting disease. Our old trouble! Finding perfectly logical reasons for our inner beliefs.

It was one morning when she was making her rounds - inseminating the gilts, as we term it in the pig world - she got no further than the fourth hut.

I was forking over some ripe vegetable compost when, from the corner of my eye, I saw several sows circling Lucy in a kind of slow walking ring. I twigged something was wrong and I moved nearer.

I was just in time to wield the pitchfork and stem their first frantic rush. it was pure aggression. Lucy shrank from their hateful screaming as I beat them off with the prongs of the fork. As I held them at bay I glanced over my shoulder to see Lucy's features twisted in a pain spasm.

It was a dangerous experience we never forgot. I rushed to her as she gently slid to the ground. The catheter in her hand was squeezed as fiercely as the pain which was gripping her muscles. I helped her back to the house and she spent the rest of the day in bed, silent and withdrawn. I was constantly on my guard with the sows after that.

It was a complete shock at the time, but it became perfectly obvious a few days later. Lucy herself was pregnant.

It seemed the answer to all our hopes. Proof enough that our decisions had been the right ones. Clearly, our venture with the pigs had been an interlude, a staging post, en route to a higher design.

In the following days Lucy did not allow herself a typical lying-in period. Perhaps we had divided the labour too precisely. There was no abandoning of our business venture, no turning back.

We owed everything to pigs. But now we had a double duty. I made a bonfire of all Lucy's charts and records. I read up on rest periods, the avoidance of toxemia in the later stages of pregnancy. Anything to bring Lucy to a successful full term.

I tried (unsuccessfully) to confine her to the house, at least in the afternoons. I hurried back each evening to pour out on her crocheted coverlet reports of the spanking condition of Florence, amusing anecdotes of Hannah's attempts to suckle her infants in turn. Several times I

The Singing Men

discovered Lucy's shoes to be saturated with dawn dew when she had left her bed to check on the behaviour of our stock.

Mrs Keogh was not informed of the impending event. That would have spoiled the element of surprise. Also, Lucy feared that her maudlin attentions might have resulted in a miscarriage, even for one so practiced as herself in the daily mechanics of birth and death.

For the last three months Mrs Keogh and her Mini were carefully excluded from Porker's Drift. Under the pretext of constructing a hardcore road to the site we were able to stave off her unwelcome visits. The last few days were idyllic. Only Lucy and I shared the intimacy of the cosy farmhouse. We were content in each other's company. Even our simple reading rarely strayed beyond the issues of the weekly *Pig Farming*.

When the moment finally arrived I was more than equal to the mechanics, pedestrian to both of us by now, of seperating mother and child.

We were obliged, of course, to disarm Mrs Keogh's inevitable fury by telephoning her immediately after the birth. As I viewed her Mini rounding the far alder copse I had a queasy vision of my role in the forthcoming confrontation.

Kevin was only several hours old and Lucy, under the white sheets, still drowsy, hardly aware of her surroundings, let alone of her mother standing in the window framed like a ghoul in the bursting sunshine. Mrs Keogh wasn't looking at her daughter or the infant. She was glaring, hate scribbled in her eyes, at me. She stalked over and her gaze of loathing was welded to my surely innocent look.

"It's not a baby!" she spat out. I looked at her, mesmerized by her yellow teeth, expecting the dentine to grind into fugitive balls of powder. "It's a PIG!", she growled into my face, keeping her voice low for Lucy's sake.

Kevin was swaddled in layers of white. His extremities were sandwiched from view between the folds. I had gone through sheer hell in the last twenty four hours. I didn't feel much like Mrs Keogh.

Lucy and I had lived in isolation, apart from our hundred pigs, the postman, and an occasional visiting lorry, for many months. I had been dreading this moment, half-believing that I might be hallucinated. That the hallucination might disappear when Lucy rose from her bed or when I came in contact with the outside world. Now Mrs Keogh had broken the spell.

Babies, as is well known, are half-formed pinkish clay, lacking definition. Mere fleshy smudges, innocent of physical persona. I had tried, with anxiety of being a first time parent, to grapple with the possibility of congenital deformity in our offspring. Before Mrs Keogh's motorised re-entrance into our lives I had examined quite minutely every inch of Kevin's body and listened to his tiny squeals.

Was I judging his little features, with its Lucy-like flattish nose, by the facial standards surrounding me every day? Could there be some aberration which, like a hair-lip, could be attended to later? I didn't remember having seen a human baby so young before. In my sheltered life they had always seemed to spring from the womb fully formed, heavily powdered, with hair, and a definitive expression.

I now marvelled at the similarities between pigs and our own kind. Kine and kind, as you might say. At birth piglets have a relatively large head. Their legs are long and their bodies are small. The exact opposite to what is found in an adult pig. They have little or no hair and need to be kept warm as they are deficient in sweat glands. The correspondence between themselves and the human baby is a common-place. Nevertheless my mind signalled to my heart that doubts existed. A picture of the duchess holding the metamorphic baby in *Alice* frequently swam before my eyes.

Mrs Keogh was prey to no such doubts. Her native intelligence and almost pathogenic hatred of me flared and led her to a conclusion which brooked neither fair discussion nor the civilised weighing of alternatives.

"My God!" she whispered, giving every word a breath to itself, "You've played us a dirty trick this time!" I could only contrive to look as unlike a confidence trickster as possible.

"I assure you, Margaret" (I tried to keep a formal edge on the emotive situation) "there is no trick, and none intended"

"But - that's a bloody *pig*!" she hissed in a subdued scream, pointing and jingling her idiotic bangles.

I have no intention of reliving the distressing scenes which followed. Her callous attitude, the sowing of seeds of distrust in the mind of a young mother. Finally, her stamping out and the blunt threat to young Kevin and myself to have us "seen to" by a "qualified practitioner". As her Mini roared away in a self-immolating flurry of granite chips I despaired of ever securing the approval she so determinedly withheld.

By the next day Lucy was in tears. It wasn't so much the small trotters - often the feet of newly-borns may be joined by web-like flanges, and a minor operation - completely safe - will correct Natures's frolic. Neither did the flat nose cause us much disquiet. Babies are often so strangely "impersonal" in infancy that we amuse ourselves in later life playing the party game of matching the photo on the hearth rug with the pompous adult we know so well.

This sort of innocent pastime may well be, as I gently reminded Lucy, accompanied by the jibes of "only a mother could love" variety. In this bantering vein I suggested that, in the words of the song "You must have been a beautiful baby etc"- young Kevin might well develop from an ungainly frog to a handsome prince in later years. At that stage I did not mention my sudden discovery of Kevin's tiny spiral tail.

When Lucy came across it, in the course of her maternal ministrations, she flung me a peculiar look of reproach. It had the same brassy hardness I had seen on Mrs Keogh's face. Why, I asked, was I perpetually placed on the defensive by those about me? Was it kinder to constantly urge the darker possibilities of fate than to lead one's partner to scan the sunlit uplands of hope?

I could appreciate her distress. Here again I could only suggest amiably that some surgical modification of the coccyx might redeem Nature's sportive non-conformity.

I must record that Lucy immediately rounded on me and accused me of being a "romantic". She had the same forthright bluntness which struck me as hideously anti-social in her mother. I had to emphasise that we should be glad that we had been gifted with a healthy young life. That perhaps - though neither of us professed an orthodox faith - counting our blessings might not be out of order.

This seemed, if anything, to deepen Lucy's gloom, and I could do little to rekindle her cheerfulness. I wondered if this could be allied to "post-natal blues" I had read about. From time to time, as my now heavier duties would allow, I peeped into the bedroom. Lucy frequently hove into an exhausted slumber. Once I spotted her sniffling and uncovering Kevin's lower torso to examine it minutely. I crept away, miserably, longing for the solace of prayers I could not utter. Lucy's happiness was all I cared about.

The next crisis was inevitably breast-feeding. With our organic outlook on life we believed that infants lost vital fluid elements as well as essential body-relationships by bottle-feeding. Unfortunately Kevin's teeth were so needle-sharp that breast-feeding was out of the question. After witnessing several tearful attempts to slake his voracious thirst, I took the van into town and entered *Mothercare*, thus breaking a vow we had made.

Two days had passed since Kevin entered our lives and it was becoming clear that we had no ordinary infant on our hands. His cheeks were pale, he slept fitfully and looked near death. By now I think we both accepted that the tail was a medical curiosty which might require hospitilisation. I rang the vet.

We agreed to place Kevin in a dog-basket near the lounge fire and when the vet arrived I would excuse Lucy's bedridden state as a temporary indisposition. He was distant on the phone and when he arrived I detected a surliness in his tone.

"Baby pig disease!" he muttered, handling Kevin rather roughly. "Bloody sugar deficiency."

I was glad that Lucy wasn't present when he took a hypodermic from his case and thrust it into Kevin's bottom. I winced as if it was my own flesh.

"Be dead in a week if you left it." The non-personal pronoun sounded especially cruel. He brought out a plastic flask. "Sow-milk substitute. Feed it this."

As he left he put his head back round the door. "I'll pop back day after tomorrow. And bring the bill. And -" he added with a sneer " - get all that talcum off its bum. What the hell d'ye think you spawned!"

I was glad to see him go. I sat in the fireside chair, thinking for a long time before I carried Kevin back to Lucy's bedroom. I briefly related what had happened. I think only Kevin slept soundly that night.

The vet returned as promised. He was less grumpy this time. For his benefit we had gone through the ritual of washing Kevin and giving him the run of the lounge. The vet presented us with an enormous bill and the advice that Kevin should get out more. He pronounced himself satisfied with Kevin's progress and ran Kevin's now stiff little tail through his fingers approvingly.

"Castration in three weeks," he said flatly, almost as if commenting on the weather. "Should have his teeth pulled as well. Want me to do it?"

Lucy turned her face to the wall to hide her tears. I said, stoney faced, that we'd let him know and led him to the back door. When I turned back Lucy had rushed in the bedroom and bolted the door.

No word from Mrs Keogh until the next day when the phone rang.

"I am in a state of shock," she said in a distinct and level voice. "Perhaps of the catatonic variety," she added, as if to edit any sympathetic response. "I haven't said anything to anybody yet. Not that I'm worried about *you*. I imagine that in *your* case certification would simply be a matter of completing the correct forms. My daughter is my sole concern. There is a good home waiting for her where she may live quietly with prospect of becoming normal again." I slammed down the reciever just as Lucy came downstairs. That was the last sort of nonsense she would want to hear. She looked drained as I took her hands.

"He"- she began, hardly able to govern her speech, " - he mentioned - cast-castration..." She lifted her face to mine. "You - you wouldn't let... would you?" For reply I kissed her full on the mouth.

During the next joyless days we were occupied with our own thoughts. On a new, higher level of mutual trust we had agreed that Kevin should be allowed to integrate himself with the rest of the herd. The innocent flush of possessive parenting had passed. I questioned Lucy gently whether she felt any pangs of maternal deprivation. She simply looked wan.

I wandered about the farm, my concentration gone, renewing straw here and there, mechanically boiling up the now redundant catheters. In fact I was really keeping an eye on young Kevin. Lucy appeared to have no stomach for her former absorbing duties. She seemed to be almost repelled by the sight of those instruments of procreation which are but the stock-in-trade of pig husbandry.

To tell you the truth, our marriage was once more entering a rocky phase. I steered the conversation away from Mrs Keogh. Lucy was ever at the window gazing forlornly at the flat expanse of the farm where the far white mice-bodies of our neglected herd ran wild in the long sweet grass. Her eyes would lighten suddenly, her lips would break in a tight remembering smile. I knew she fancied that she had caught sight of Kevin and was following his small dashing form - anxious to reassure herself that he suffered no teasing from his peer group, nor bullying from the sows.

Strong invisible bonds still linked the three of us. Though we had silently accepted different worlds we enjoyed a quiet sense of equilibrium. Sometimes as I walked between the huts I would sense a bright pink face peering at me from behind a wooden post. I never turned around. To do so would have given encouragement to hopes which only existed in a past dream.

Lucy became withdrawn and sat for days in the window-seat. Her response to me was no longer corporeal, merely half-grudging monosyllables. The farm could never be run as a one-man business. I reluctantly placed it in the "For Sale" columns of *Pig Farming*. We had several enquiries and at last a definite offer.

The time came when we had but a week in which to leave the farm. I was awake early each morning, making sure that everything was to hand for the new owner. I had left Lucy in bed one morning when she suddenly gave me the slip. I returned to the house for my mid-morning break, creeping upstairs to kiss the mist of sleep from her eyes. She was no longer there. I searched the house starting from the top. She was not to be found. I guessed she had slipped outside.

I heard the screams before I had even crossed the yard. In fact I nearly tripped over Kevin who was usually hanging about the back door waiting for a hug. I recognised the terror in his face.

I wouldn't have thought that such an inhuman noise could come from Lucy's throat and my hand went instinctively for the pitchfork as I remembered the time before. Kevin ran before me as if he was leading me to the terrible scene.

The long pallid bodies of the sows were gathered like great sausage spokes on a giant wheel. At the centre of the wheel their snouts were playing with what looked like a large red rag doll.

My cheeks were cold with sweat as I grasped the situation. I charged in with the fork like some demented gladiator, swinging stabbing blows at the sows and shouting myself hoarse. Little Kevin ran to the edge of the field completely terrified.

It took me the best part of five minutes before I fended off the slashing of their dripping jaws. Lucy had clearly been dead very soon after they had brought her down.

I knelt, my knees braced apart and shaking, beside Lucy's body, still grasping the blooded pitch fork. I seemed to see and hear nothing, until I felt Kevin nuzzling my thigh. And until I heard the rising roar of Mrs Keogh's Mini.

I no longer ask myself, as I did at the beginning, who is to blame? Telling this story has been cathartic. The psychiatrist was clinically ambivalent but that is no more than I expected. I am quite sure that we took pigs too seriously. Who can blame a pig for that? And now, for myself, the truth is locked up inside a small pig, soon to be slaughtered.

The warders think I shall no longer hang after all. "It's the funny farm for you, mate," they say.

Reec-Ret

"The great thing is not to get under anyone's feet."

It was Martyn who said it, not Margaret his wife. It was their joke. Like the sensible people they were, they had been through the *Preparing for Retirement* business long before Martyn experienced the actual event, and without the benefit of a college course. She stood now on the collapsible stool wiping down some shelves. He stood two feet lower down ready to catch her and feeling like a naughty boy playing truant from school, and wondering how the new graduate Chambers was coping with the accounts for headquarters.

"You said it!" said Margaret. She gave him a flick with the wet duster. All day he had felt as though his true self had been nudged aside and, like an astral photographer, he was recording quite neutrally happenings which did not connect with him. During that first afternoon he had already seen Margaret in various unusual situations, battling with the checkout girl to load her stuff before the invoice chattered out of the till, exchanging chaff with the window cleaner, in total command of a battery of highly expensive, technical household appliances.

They told him not to fret about the office. That retirement meant a new career. Freedom, reflection, wisdom, leisure, these were all his to enjoy. It wasn't that easy. You had to carve out something else.

On the Tuesday he went to the supermarket. Margaret insisted. It was amazing how long shopping took. Not to get under each other's feet. At first he devised a kind of time and motion study. He divided the shopping list into two by simply tearing it in half. Margaret took one half, himself the other. This didn't quite work. They kept passing each other, rather self-consciously in the middle, at Cheeses and Yoghurts.

Next time he made out a proper list before they left the house. He split the items in walking order, so they could each do half in separate trolleys and keep all the chilled cabinet purchases cooler together in one trolley. Unfortunately he found on his list several items of feminine hygiene which required Margaret's presence in the Toiletries aisle.

"What we really need is a multi-dimensional matrix." Which brought him a sympathetic moue from her.

They could eliminate automatically, of course, the stacks of Pet Foods, Sweets and Children Requisities. But collecting the items separately could be rather dull, and they both kept thinking of things not on their list but not daring to buy lest it was on the other's. Neither was there the intimacy of comparing suggestions. Consultation and decisions on types of soaps, magazines, Italian sauces, were lost. After a week or so, they dispensed with the eco-efficiency benefits of division of labour and went round together.

They even played games. Martyn was acutely aware of men of his own age and situation. When he spotted one he would nudge Margaret and whisper (sometimes say out loud) "Another Reec-ret!" This was Martynspeak for Recently Retired. You could tell them, particularily those who had held supervisory positions. They seemed to fall into two categories: those with faces like pumped-up tomatoes, and those of paler hue sporting grey hair and grey faces covered with a patina of pre-death frosting. It was a knife-edge question as to which type would die first. They usually wore tightly buttoned executive jackets above which their faces froze in a permanent glare. They held up tins of chopped tomatoes and scowled at them critically through steel-rimmed spectacles as if they were sales graphs. Their wives were clamped to their sides, usually pushing the trolley. It was clear that Recently Retired Husbands were keen to bring much needed business expertise into the feminine sphere. Sometimes they would catch their wives in some sudden aberration of mind or mental waywardness. At such times they would issue audible reprimands at such female indecision and cast about triumphal glances to seek the rapport and approval of any passing male.

The type was not confined to executives who had recently been deprived of command. Male manual workers exhibited the same alienated stiffness, as if they had been tricked and had stumbled into the ladies lavatory. "Reec-ret?" Martyn would utter with a quizzical air as he passed them. The man in question might look up startled, anxious to greet a fellow sufferer, then lose interest assuming he had misheard, whilst Margaret stifled her laughter.

Margaret enjoyed this game. Martyn and the other men were adapting to a largely feminine world. She knew its rewards and its limitations. At the same time she felt a responsibility to introduce him to cooking, the choosing of furniture and fabrics, decorating, the art of vacuum cleaning, toilet swabbing, and, of course, shopping. We all have a social duty, she reminded him, we are social animals. They had decided quite early on not to bury themselves in the country but to keep alive in the social mix of town.

Tuesday was their day for supermarket shopping. And it was on that day that Martyn was almost buried under a collapsing pyramid of baked beans. The young couple rushed to help him to his feet and to rescue their tiny daughter who had caused the pile to fall. Martyn was not hurt, only a grazed leg, but the chaos was spectacular. The young mother was very concerned and Martyn felt a surprising strength in her arm as she helped him up. The husband dusted down his pretty blonde daughter. Margaret said afterwards that he looked as if a beanbomb had hit him and she wished she had a camera. An assistant verified that no lasting harm had occurred. Martyn was gallantly concerned about the child who began almost immediately to restore the stack of tins to child height.

The following Tuesday they met the young couple with their child at precisely the same spot. There was a great deal of laughter and an elaborate steering clear of the stack. A moment's pause, during which they briefly relived the incident of the previous week. Martyn, it seemed, had been christened the Bean Man, and was the topic of untiring conversation and analysis in the Morris's household.

Sally, the child, enquired wistfully about Martyn's leg and even attempted to roll up his trouser leg to carry out her own inspection. Martyn must have seemed to her like a long grey tree. Her button face appeared to him as a newly opened flower. The Morris's were a bright young couple, easy to talk to. They had a way of not making any "allowances" for age, or sex, or occupation. Martyn felt strangely flattered to be treated by them as an equal. Of not being an object of "respect", or of wisdom and veneration. He looked forward to seeing them next week.

The thing which impressed Martyn the most was the strange feeling when Sally's hand was on his leg. It was almost a sensuous brushing touch hardly touching the hair that he felt when the tiny fingers reached his shin. In that moment when he looked down it seemed that only he and Sally existed, and the others became miasmic jostling onlookers, their voices crushed to nothing as when the volume of a radio is turned down. The child's hair framed features which out-kewpied any doll he had ever seen. Her look of concern concentrated her mouth, her large eyes, her strained features.

Their meetings became a regular Tuesday thing, and when Mrs Morris spoke sharply to Sally about putting things from the shelves in her trolley, Martyn experienced a sharp pointed pleasure which poked and raked at the division in the small family. He salved his own conscience by talking to Mr Morris quite animatedly about next Saturday's prospects for the local rugby team. That evening a voice not quite his own spoke to Margaret over tea.

"The Morris's are new, I think, in the town. Perhaps they haven't made many friends yet,"

Margaret looked up. "What makes you say that? Young attractive couple with a baby like that. they probably ensnare friends like puppy owners."

His eyes wandered directionless over the evening paper. "Ensnare." Unusual verb. Not a Margaret word at all.

"Well, him at work all day, and Mrs Morris keeping the house. I just wondered if it would help if we offered to do a shop for them?"

She smiled. "I seem to have convinced you shopping takes a mountain of time."

He was surprised to find himself proposing this when they met the Morris's next Tuesday. As they would call and pick up her list in the car and drop the shopping later, why couldn't they look after Sally as well? The nights were getting dark and the shopping could be done during the day when it was quieter. Mrs Morris was dismissive at first. But they were relieved to see that this was nothing to do with the fact that they were an "older couple". When she agreed it made them both feel young at heart to be accepted like this. As Margaret said, the young keep the old from growing older. Martyn could think of nothing else until the afternoon.

The whole episode went off well. There was no doubt that Mrs Morris had a burden lifted from her. On the way back they did not linger for tea or a chat. There was no point in spoiling their good deed by forcing the Morris's to entertain them. They promised to do the same next week.

It was clear to Martyn that Sally was extremely happy with them. Margaret made a remark about him being a "shadow grandfather" and making up for the children they never had. Sally was happy to watch children's television on his knee, and she had a peculiar practice of reaching up with the hand not occupied with thumb-sucking and rubbing his ear, while her eyes were fixed on the screen. This had the same effect as her hand on his leg on the first occasion. His slight worry about this cracked into laughter when she suddenly said, nailing him with her melting brown eyes, "I love you!" It took Margaret by surprise and she made some remark about him keeping two women on the trot.

It was perfectly natural to offer to baby-sit for the Morris's, and one which was taken up readily. There were some instructions about story rationing and permitted number of biscuits, and the teeth cleaning ritual. Martyn wrote these down on the first occasion. It was important to show the Morris's that they were taking seriously this new source of their pleasure. Sally looked even more fascinating in her nightgown than in the anorak.

The first night Margaret wandered about the Morris's house taking in their holiday photos and the kind of CD's and books they bought. There was no doubt she approved. They put Sally to bed together the first night. Then Margaret suggested that she was too excited at the thought of monopolising the attention of two adults. Martyn, as the most competent story teller, was elected to be the last to see her off to sleep.

Mr Morris's attitude was interesting. Morris, he noticed, was not in the habit of cuddling Sally. Access to his knee was often barred by the newspaper or by official documents brought home from work. When Martyn mentioned this to Margaret she said perhaps Sally was deprived of male bonding and that he, Martyn, was making up for this. It was comforting to have theoretical basis for the attraction he felt. He could respond confidently to the amused look on Morris's face when Sally flew into his arms whenever they arrived. Morris seemed to him permanently harassed by the need to succeed in his job. He insisted that Sally called Martyn "Uncle Martyn" to preserve respect. For some reason this annoyed Martyn though it was preferable to "Grandad".

When he found that Sally dominated his thoughts in the few days before they were due to babysit, Martyn tried to analyse his feelings. There was, of course, the mixture of innocence and helpless appeal of her doll-like face, the sense that his situation was very similar to hers. Days filled with nothing but the search for interest and pleasure, no pressure to undertake tasks. A second chilhood, in fact. Often he glanced across to Margaret when they were alone and he saw the same feminine movements, the same sexless confidence, he saw in Sally. It kept him awake at night. In Margaret and Sally he saw the same looks and gestures of sensuous power and unconscious allure. He had read about the cosmic role of a male and female and the theory that man's life quest is but a journey from the womb and a return to it, of the apartness and mystery of women - briskly, of course, denied by Margaret. Yet there was some hint of a siren-quality in the little girl's stare.

Margaret seemed quite unconcerned. She came into the room once when he was changing Sally's nappy. Her reaction was quite indifferent. Children were children. It wasn't as if she had ever caught him wearing women's clothes or anything. At one time she had even laughed at the sight of him hugging Sally and made some sly references to "Cupid with his amorous dart." She extracted as much humour as possible from the situation. He was piqued, and yet relieved that he he could discover no kind of jealousy there.

Mrs Morris's attitude was, he suspected, cautious. She was used to a masculine, he might even say macho, relationship where male/female tasks were sharply defined. She would have been astonished had she known Martyn changed Sally's nappy. He was irritated to think that it was a secret kept from her. Sometimes he wished that they had never met the Morris's, and that Sally had not been the cause of disturbing thoughts. A psychiatrist would have had a field day. It had been so uncomplicated at the office. He had kept his hands strictly off even slightly sullied typists, unlike some of his male colleagues who had played with their superior spending power and their prerogative of preferment.

He warned himself that he must keep a distance between himself and Sally. There was too much in the newspapers about sexual perversions of all kinds. He allowed Margaret the privilege of bathing and changing her and stopped coaxing her on to his knee. He permitted a note of disinterest to overtake him until he found himself in a depressive mood.

It was the morning when he received a cheque from the insurance company - a little surprising as he had forgotten the maturity date of the endowment. A fatuous letter accompanied the cheque to the effect that he might like to take out another, shorter term policy. He showed it to Margaret. With his comfortable pension and the assets they had built up there was no sensible reason for such an investment so late in life.

The following day he reflected on this and it produced a kind of gloom and the feeling that another portcullis had clanged down behind him. He was nearing what certain clergymen might refer to as the "twilight of his days". It suddenly occured to him that it might be a reason for his feelings for Sally? Was he trying to be part of a new life when he was approaching the end of his own? Did he want to "impress" himself on her memory, leave an imprint of himself behind? Such foolishness was the stuff of life.

Martyn had frequently woken up in the early hours when the fantasies of his dreams had led his real life by the nose and tweaked it through the corridors of horror and magic. Now he found that such absurdities were creeping into his wakening life. Margaret remained solidly and soberly feminine, his rock and positive anchor in the world of their possessions.

The Morris's had loaned them a child's safety seat for the back of the car when they took Sally to the supermarket, and when Margaret pronounced herself "under the weather" he had no hesitation in taking Sally himself.

He found himself driving across town, taking the usual route to his old office. There was a supermarket nearby to which he and Margaret had never been. He felt almost light-headed as he parked the car and lifted Sally from the back. He chose one of the special baby trolleys and placed Sally in its seat where her face was endlessly smiling at his. She was facing him the whole way and her eyes were fixed on him like some beguiling badges. He thought whimsically how she might be repulsed by him in a dozen years when her maturer thoughts on standards of attractiveness had been formed. As he pushed the trolley down the aisle he thought back to his youth, when he would have given his right arm for a smile from anyone as beautiful as Sally, to feel her pure breath on his cheek and to lock his gaze on her clear chestnut eyes.

He went past Pickles and Preserves putting things in the trolley without consulting his list. He allowed Sally to lean over and drop some nonsensical things in. The supermarket called itself a hypermarket and it was vast. The fluourescent lights marched in rows away from him, it seemed almost to the horizon like gleaming swords of some great army. One might lose oneself in here. If one were accidently locked in one could survive, perhaps for years, glimpsing the sky through the distant windows and sensing the wind by the blown litter hammering at the automatic doors. Sally gazed steadily into his eyes and her chatter was frequent but not distracting. He realized that this was the first time he had really been alone with Sally.

It seemed but a short time before they were seated in the small restaurant of the store. The effort of pushing Sally had tired him a little. He had played the same Reec-ret game that he played with Margaret. Sally had regarded him knowingly and had even laughed in the right places. Now he fed her an illicit plate of spaghetti hoops and a cream cake. He had read somewhere that the proportion of laughing to smiling, in minutes per hour per child, is unbelievably large. In adults the proportion is entirely reversed. He was now doing his best to correct the latter.

Sally seemed quite determined to resist any thoughts of an afternoon nap. He put her in the baby seat and wheeled her back into the shopping area. She gazed up at him with her wide lustrous eyes, her chubby mouth pressed into a voluptuous smile. As he passed the delicatessen counter they waved to the assistants. He noticed that one of the assistants, after waving back, said something to her companion. They moved on and he looked at his watch. He noted, without concern, that they had been in the shop over four hours.

The place had filled up and he was beginning to feel sleepy himself with the brightness of the ceiling lights. Sally was pointing out excitedly the displays they had passed before. The trolley was almost full and Martyn felt with a happy idiocy that at some point he would have to sort it out and put things back on the shelves. But not yet. He was dazed. He could even believe he was bewitched by Sally into a kind of silly dreamworld where nonsense ruled - a world of stark reality where matronly ideas of behaviour were toppled and sober-faced mandarins were goaded into hysterical comedy. He stopped for a moment and mopped his face with a handkerchief. He hadn't experienced this dizziness before. He bent down and leaned his forehead on the trolley handle. Sally put her hand to his face and stroked his ear. He remained like that for a minute or so before he felt a hand on his arm. An old face looked into his.

"Feeling a bit off it are we?" It was a man's face, dusty with age and lined with the grooves of a life of work.

He peered up at the man, not quite in command of himself yet. "Are you a recently retired person by any chance?"

The man looked startled and began to move away back to where his wife stood anxiously with their trolley.

Another man took his place. "Can I help?"

Martyn straightened up. He was looking into the face of Chambers, a young inquisitive face to which he had bid goodbye only a few weeks ago.

He felt himself smile and was conscious that Sally was smiling with him.

"Have headquarters accepted those accounts yet?"

"It's Mr Meadows, isn't it?" said Chambers. Then suddenly Chambers was pulled away.

Martyn looked sideways to see the brown check dress of an assistant.

"Do you not feel well, sir?"

He looked up. All the shoppers and Chambers were gone. The aisle seemed to be filled with men in blue shirts. It could have been part of his dream. He stared at them and straightened up before two of the policemen took his arms and another lifted Sally from the baby seat of the trolley. As they hustled him down the aisle he had time to see

Margaret's drawn face and her hand stretched out to him. The Morris's stood by a stack of baked bean tins. The expression on their faces was one of worry and wonderment as Sally was handed back to them.

Water Baby

I'm sure Stephen didn't really mean to drown Freda and me.

I first noticed his symptoms in the fifties. I don't think Freda was sufficiently into child psychology, although she was a social worker. Her courses and conferences hadn't prepared her for this sort of thing.

It was a family holiday. We had been chivvied onto the beach by the landlady as soon as the breakfast cruet had been snatched away. A desperate scenario. Seagulls chewing sodden crisps. Ice-cream all down my trouser leg. It was raining like hell and all the bus shelters were full. But where could you go on a day like this except back home? After a bit it eased up. Stephen played in the sand. He didn't mind the cold. He dug happily while I read the newspaper and Freda knitted in her solitary way.

At first I thought it was a series of sandcastles dug by other people which, by a trick of the eye, seemed to link up left and right of our sun trap. They stretched away in terraces back to where a stream issued from the bottom of the seawall. It looked as if the beach had erupted in a leprous rash of over-filled sand cups.

I put down the paper and straightened up slowly to disperse the stiffness in my knees. Stephen's tiny castles were filled to the ramparts with water. They seemed to pivot in a triangle with their apex at our suntrap. I looked back to where the stream began. As I swivelled I caught sight of Stephen in the rear. There was a hell-bent look stamped on his little face. I was about to wave to him when he suddenly leaned forward and churned with his spade, thrusting at a particular ring of sand. The seconds seemed to slow and the air bristled as if metallic clouds were giving up static. Then it dawned on me. Stephen had released the first small torrent of water from a kind of header dam.

What he had been doing over the last two hours I saw only too well. First one castle crumbled. Then, by a domino effect, another. The cascade fed a third and so on. Each castle was artfully placed so the rush of water boosted the next. I just had time to drag Freda from the suntrap before a sizeable flood hit us.

All the time I kept an eye on Stephen expecting a child's laughter at this discomfiture of parental authority. His face held nothing but a dull stare. For some reason this lack of expected response infuriated me and I chased him all over the beach while Freda wrung out her Fair Isle jumper. She wasn't very impressed. And my angina hunted about fearfully in my chest.

We didn't chastise Stephen physically. Freda and I had agreed things like this before we started family planning. After all, Stephen was still a child. And it *was* supposed to be a holiday. Also, I felt a queer tingle of pride in what he had done. He was a late developer as fat as speech was concerned, a bit of a loner. He never confided in either of us, about bullying at school, or the puzzling concepts of the adult world.

"It's his way of revealing his intellect and his preferred instincts," I suggested.

"I expect he's trying to win our approval," grumbled Freda.

I sensed that she'd 'given him up' long ago, sometime during Stephen's babyhood, her period of 'enforced house arrest' as she called it. She wanted something average and normal. Like a Fair Isle jumper.

I couldn't help admiring his artistry. The whole concept was so far removed from a child's teeming and pouring. His mind, I realised, was dominated by the concept of water. From then on, I continued to observe Stephen. I noted his lack of eye contact with people, but also the torch-like intensity of his obsession with water. He would play long and quietly in the bath, not because it delayed bedtime, but for the pure joy of shuddering with ecstacy when water slid through his fingers. He was simply entranced by the shimmering jelly of its twitching surface He would drag a stool and stand on it over the sink, running the tap and staring manically at its thin silver rope caught in a sunshaft. Sometimes I crept up and gently held his slim trunk in my palms. It was vibrating uncontrollably. Once he turned round to see if I shared his joy.

When he grew into his matchstick teens, I thought he would take naturally to swimming and aqua sports. Not a bit. He was not interested in teams or competition. He was simply fascinated by water, the plasticity of its forms, its noises and weight, the awful power of its moving mass. His only youthful hobby was fishing. He would stand like a lord on the river bank drawing its secrets to his net. He fished where the water moved fastest, rapids for trout, weirs for barbel. Once I accompanied him on a muggy June day. The air lay like a heavy poultice above our heads before the high summer pomps exploded upstream in a tremendous downpour. Water poured down our valley and the river burst its banks even before darts of rain thrashed its surface.

Stephen stopped fishing to watch. Each stalk of grass was festered blackly with insects escaping the rising flood. In the purple light roach skittered, maddened by the harvest of earthworms coiling from the drowned vegetation. Soon the swollen waters stretched tightly over the valley. Finally I had to drag him away as he protested in a heathen outcry.

Whenever I broached the subject of water his face lapsed into a sideways reverie as if I had tripped a primal memory scar. Some years later we took a Scottish holiday. Our moorland walks bored him until we came across the blue-black tarns and burns. There he swiftly fashioned locks and dams from tumbled stones, whilst we ate our sandwiches watching his progress with shaking heads and oblique matching smiles. If there was a water sprite or dryad about, it seemed to be working its impish way with him as heather and needle dross hurried to fill the gaps in his strategically placed rocks, before he finally slipped the key rock which loosened the torrent.

Freda explained to me that water entranced all children. No wonder, she added prosaically, when they had so recently spent nine months in the amniotic fluid,

At school physics was his main subject. He tried for marine biology, but found himself on an Honours course in civil engineering. No employment problems. He went abroad after that, head-hunted by a famous firm of international engineers. He never came back to England.

He kept in touch with us via a stream of world souvenirs, batik work from the East Indies, brassware from India, miniature assegais from Africa. We would meet him again, I felt sure, when I took early retirement and we thought about world travel.

Freda was enthusiastic and our first step came by way of Stephen's invitation. He firm had contracted for a hydro scheme on the Watusi River. The official opening of the dam was a year away, in March. Stephen's area of work had been to create the finished blueprints for the coffer dam, a vital, though subsidiary part of the whole operation. Could we make it, he asked?

We flew out a few days before the opening. The smells, the tastes, the sounds of Africa! We picked up a light plane from Lilongwe and skimmed low over the red, shrivelled landscape, with the occasional paint-green chip nestling in the giant thighs of its hills. Stephen, our son, would bring fresh green life to the whole of this burnt-out land.

He seemed older. Freda fussed about, inspecting his kit like a sergeant-major. In his photos he had been laughing, arms linked with the construction gang, tanned flesh to the waistband of his shorts, standing in a crowd of camera-shy natives. Not now. When he saw us, his eyes reached back into their sockets. The searching dust of Africa had settled into wrinkles and the loose skin on his neck a lizard might have discarded. He still flinched at intimacy. He was now a grown man and I felt a desperation that he would never confide in us during our lifetimes.

"Nothing's the matter," he said without much conviction.

"This country's getting to you" I said. I wiped the red sore band on my forehead. "Low altitudes are no use to a European in this country."

He looked away with his curious apartness. He became animated only when he pulled out the thin drawer of blueprints and explained the enormous pressure of billions of gallons of river water. My mind flew back to the beach and the Scottish highlands.

The day before the opening we all went in the safari truck up to the hills with Askaris standing guard on the running boards. Stephen explained the catchment area and pointed out the parts that would be flooded and the irrigation network. His voice was high and his speech trembled. As we drove along my eyes were more on him than on the dried snakeskins of the river beds we passed. Tribespeople along the road were covered with our red dust as we sped along. They carried sugar cane, firewood, and huge precious cans of water. Stephen ignored them, commenting only on the technical miracle beginning tomorrow, which might put an end to this primitive existence.

That night I stared at the coin of the moon through my mosquito net. The mozzies buzzed on the other side anxious for their blood meal. I was just dropping off when I heard footsteps outside. They hit the concrete path in a way that didn't sound like bare feet. Something made me get up quickly.

Outside the bungalow, I saw the figure some yards in front going down the path, skirting the native portakabins and making for the transport compound. As we went through, the ghostly shapes of great earth-moving equipment towered on each side, paralysed without their human operators. By the time we were on the approach road to the dam I was gasping like the old man I was, but Stephen kept his pace, striding forward as if on a mission. I had a job to keep him in sight as he doubled through the complex. My fears shaped up as he marched rapidly to the control pavilion. I fought the hot lump in my chest. I was almost running now and my flapping bedroom slippers must have been quite audible to him. He never once looked back.

When he reached the gantry I was only a few yards behind. A night-shift worker, moon-white overalls springing from under his black face, touched his forehead in recognition and moved to let us pass. Stephen took the catwalk two steps at a time and leaped smartly on to the console platform. I had that third stage crushing sensation in my chest which definitely signals an attack - but I heaved myself forward in a last effort as Stephen smacked down several electrical switches in rotation. And when his hand finally hovered over the flume button, I was able to clamp his wrist in my hand. My scream racketed through the girder braces like an eldritch shriek.

His face turned towards me pale with sleep, but his eyes were pin-bright and sharp-coned with hatred. I screwed his hand back from the button.

"No-oo!" I screamed with all my force into his face.

He was shuddering like a man in a fever. I now held his hand as I had once held his tiny shivering body. Then for some strange reason, not born of my mind alone, I cried: "Stephen, we love you. We *love* - !" His hands dropped to his side. He was cold to my touch and greasy with sleep and sweat. I don't think in his conscious mind he heard me. In a way I was glad. It wouldn't be a source of embarrassment to us both when he woke.

When we got back to his hut I quickly sprayed his room with a knock-down canister and tucked him into the truckle bed. I bore down on his shaking shoulders but when I put the mossi net over him it was like drawing a veil over the smudged relaxed features of a baby.

Next morning, after the furnace of an African dawn, but before the sky had assumed its white-hot grin, the wife of the Head of Overseas Operations lifted her lacy gloved finger as we gathered round. In a tentative feminine gesture she touched the red flume button on the panel. A second later there was a roar and a great white cockatoo of foam sprang from the smooth wall of the dam.

Freda clapped vigorously with both hands upraised. She looked suddenly proud to have mothered her son. As I gripped his arm tightly Stephen turned his head and looked at me, for once directly into my eyes. I grinned at him wildly. Admiration for his achievements with water must have shone out of my face. He smiled back as if his body had come to the end of a journey and shed a great weight.

Then his gaze went back to the thundering furry spout, and he cheered his applause like a child, as heartily as anyone in that sea of sparkling cries.

The New Queen

Aristide angled her cigarette holder and arranged herself in the mirror beside the telephone. She prepared her arms-length voice to ring Brenda. Brenda was really too wholesome for close comfort. She reminded Aristide of a cottage loaf freshly prised from the oven. Clearly, people like Brenda were destined to assist other people.

Aristide sipped her iced gin and gazed at the silken sheen of her legs. Few would guess that a woman like herself was the begetter of Fuzzy Bee. She looked grimly at the pizza-sized colour blow-up of Fuzzy hanging, a laughing idiot face, above the word-processor. Mothers who bought the Bee Books would no doubt imagine her as a speccy bun-like individual curled in an armchair like a couple of upholstered car tyres, peering through pebble glasses and scratching out Fuzzy's loathsome adventures with a quill.

With a pseudonym like Candice Comfrey they might well be forgiven. It was the name Frank, their agent, had chosen - part of her image. Frank had recently signalled it was time for another bee prank. Another 32-page moral message to Fuzzy fan tots. *Fuzzy Bee Afloat! Fuzzy Bee Makes Friends! Fuzzy Bee Abroad!* The exclamation marks must surely by now have completely superseded full stops in the minds of infants everywhere. Never mind the compulsory capital letters!

Aristide pushed a languid paw towards the phone. Then she drew back and poured herself another gin. She liked her cottage in the country to have all the urban amenities. She picked up the phone.

"That you, Brenda?"
A confirmatory squawk sounded from the other end.

"Another bee in his bonnet! Frank's been on the blower again. He's aiming for one a month. Bloody slave-driver!"

Brenda sounded gutted, as if she had just been woken up and had the telephone thrust down her throat.

"*Fuzzy Bee Goes to France.* How's your French? Never mind. Just keep drawing the pictures."

A strangled buzz dribbled from the receiver.

"Well you can put something French in! Oh I don't know - game of boules - bunch of onions - blokes in berets..."

It sounded as if Brenda was having difficulty with her imagination again.

"Oh, God! It's just struck me! Frank will probably want me to go to Paris to sign copies."

There was another gargling sound, perhaps of envy, from Brenda.

"Anyway," Aristide said, "I'll send the text."

She put down the phone and flooded her jaw with gin. Really, Brenda was the bloody limit! Initially it had been a hell of a wrench to get her off bunnies and on to bees. Frank had worked on her unmercifully. For the first six months all her bees had looked like bunnies until she, Aristide, had suggested the goo-goo eyes, and the single white tooth leaping from the red hell of Fuzzy's mouth (a straight lift from Mickey Mouse). She had helped to create her own monster.

Aristide sucked greedily at the pool of gin sloshing in her mouth. Frank had suggested something more educational. *Fuzzy Bee Meets Maths*, *Fuzzy Bee Sorts Out Science*. The parents actually buy the books, he advised, play on their sense of educational guilt.

It was amazing how Brenda actually resembled a Bee, particularly when she was knitting. She reminded Aristide of an insect rubbing its mandibles (or whatever they sported) together. Her conversation was more of a buzz than an articulation. Only the wings were missing. Not only that - she actually appeared to be colour blind. Aristide had to suggest the stripey vest for Fuzzy.

Fuzzy Bee Goes To France it would be. No, *Fuzzy Bee Flies To France*. Godammit, the creature had wings! Two pairs, hadn't it? She switched on the word-processor and gazed at the wall behind, at the grinning monstrous bee face Brenda had drawn. It took a minute to twist her mouth into a clinically insane guffaw like Fuzzy's. Then she was off, and her pearl-shod finger-tips smacked the keys with gusto.

Afterwards she pared down the whole text to cut out any words over two syllables and anything that could remotely be described as Politically Incorrect. Brenda had already been told not to put any English words into illustrations to cut the cost of adapting captions to foreign markets. Frank was very strict on that.

Although she hated it, she was satisfied with her work and she stretched out her arms like a great basket handle above her head. This time it had all come right quickly. What she called a "half bottle book".

She made herself a cup of black coffee and put the print-out into a jiffy bag addressed to Brenda.

On the shelf above sat the growing stack of Fuzzy Bee books. It grew by half an inch with each additional one. She thought of the years ahead and how she had dreamed of becoming a famous romantic novelist until she had accidently (well, through Cedric really) stumbled on her talent for writing for children. When, if ever, would the mothers of the nation become terminally nauseated with Fuzzy Bee?

She had come to loathe Cedric after their divorce, in a comfortable, almost pleasurable way. Contrasted with her feelings before the divorce when, strangely enough, she had quite liked him. There had been too many romantic women who wanted to take the short further step to becoming published romantic women by hounding the willing Cedric. When Cedric turned her into a tiny tots' authoress with a wave of his publisher's wand, he had side-lined her in a world of his making, and destroyed the woman she wanted to be.

As part of the settlement he had given her this cottage, Bee Cottage, with roses round the door, an unhygienic thatched roof, even a couple of beehives in the garden. It seemed idyllic at the time. A local man saw to the bees, cleaned them and pollinated them, or something.

Aristide took down the last book, *Fuzzy Bee Goes To School*. She looked wistfully at the first one in the line, *Fuzzy Bee is Born*. She turned the pages. Brenda's illustrations had become more garish - a touch of red here, some ginger whiskers there. Fuzzy had started off quite like a bee. Now he was a cartoon, a caricature.

She compared the pictures on the front covers. Really, allowing for the fact that Fuzzy had obviously aged from infancy, he didn't resemble a bee at all. His legs had acquired muscles, his lips were now fuller and redder. There was even a suggestion of a bosom. He - or was it a she? - pranced in a little tutu skirt. And the dewy eyelashes? Aristide stared. There was a curious familiarity about the bee pictures in last month's gruesome little tale.

Her hand reached again for the bottle of gin. She needed to steady herself. Something strange here. She sipped slowly. Then it came with a jolt. Fuzzy was beginning to look like Brenda! The idea had beeen born a few minutes ago. Just sprang out of her unconscious - but the other way round - it was *Brenda* who was growing like Fuzzy. She took another sip. That was it! Brenda was becoming more like Fuzzy! Brenda was subtly changing places with Fuzzy. Was it deliberate? Was it a wish fulfilment? Did Brenda realize?

She grabbed the telephone. Then she put it down quickly. If

Brenda was acting unconsciously, we might be talking psychiatrists. On the other hand, if Brenda knew, there was no point in telling her, and it might signal a more devious approach. Had Frank noticed? Then she realized that he had never actually met Brenda. Aristide had negotiated all the contracts. Even Cedric had never met Brenda. None of the readers - or anybody else - had ever met Brenda. She never went to signings. Aristide had only met her once, in Harrods, before Christmas, for afternoon tea and to get her signature on the contract. Suddenly the future seemed horrific.

There could be deeper psychological explanations. Brenda, tired of playing second fiddle, merely an illustrator, was trying, perhaps unconsciously, to present herself to the world through her art, to leave an impression - like a child writing its name in wet concrete.

The telephone rang. It was Cedric.

"Thought I might catch you at the cottage," he drawled in his rotten publisher's voice. "Long time, no tea. How's about a tot together. Compare notes."

"Oh, it's you. 'Fraid I'm rather beesy - er, busy - at the moment Cedric."

There was a silence as if Cedric had suddenly sniffed a split infinitive. "You sound a bit boozy. Haven't been at the nectar again?"

"There is something. Have you noticed anything about the bee books?"

"Never touch them if I can help it. Leave it to Frank."

"I mean about the illustrations?"

"Darling, a bee is a bee is a bee, right? Besides, Brenda Wotsit's a marvellous illustrator."

She rang off impatiently. There wasn't much left in the bottle now. She must ring Brenda and have it out.

She arranged that Brenda should come to the cottage and chat about the foreign goings-on of Fuzzy Bee and how much "foreignness" the tiny tots could stomach per book. They would start with France, establish a bridgehead in Germany, then knock off the rest of the world over the next year or so, avoiding trouble spots like Bosnia and Somalia. Then Aristide might work the conversation round to this business of Fuzzy's metamorphosis.

As she came through the door, the first thing that Aristide noticed was Brenda's hat. It was several geological epochs out of date and sported two drooping stems of ostrich herl. They looked like antennae. Two multi-cut jewels, one on either side of its straw base, semaphored at the table light. Mercifully, Brenda removed it, but only to reveal dark, furry hair parted in the middle. When she smiled Aristide gasped as Brenda uncovered a single tooth jutting from her lower jaw. She remembered it was several dental disasters sort of huddled together. Aristide helped her to remove the heavy top coat, unseasonal in this summer heat, and was startled to see a black and orange striped jersey emerge clasping Brenda's rotund little form.

"Tea? Scones and jam?" ventured Aristide.

"Honey, if you have it," said Brenda with a Fuzzy-type smile.

"No problemo," murmured Aristide. There could be little mistake now, she thought, as Brenda sat down and crossed her legs. I would recognise those bottle legs and the bobble knees anywhere. Those are bees' knees! She decided to adopt the Approach Direct.

"Glancing through the books the other day, I noticed how much Fuzzy's appearance had changed, Brenda," she opened.

"Changed?" buzzed Brenda.

"Children are such conservative creatures," said Aristide. "Take Rupert Bear, for instance. He's hardly changed since the thirties."

Brenda's eyes grew round and mischievous. "Do you know," she confided, "I sometimes draw Fuzzy's face from my own."

"Aha!" said Aristide. They were getting somewhere at last.

"To factualise the expressions," said Brenda. "I look in the mirror and screw my face up - for example, when Fuzzy's been especially naughty and put his hand - er pad, I suppose - into the salt instead of the sugar to taste it."

"I remember that," said Aristide, "Book Fourteen, *Fuzzy Bee Begins Baking*."

Brenda had screwed up her face to demonstrate.

"Sometimes I actually think I am Fuzzy!" said Brenda. Her plum-pudding head dipped towards the honey. Aristide smiled. This was going to be easier than she hoped!

"Actually, I thought Fuzzy was beginning to resemble you - if you don't mind the observation," said Aristide. There! It was out!

"And that Fuzzy had lost most of his - her? - I don't even know the sex! - bee-like qualities," added Aristide.

"Ah," said Brenda, wagging what seemed like a proboscis but turned out to be a finger held near her face. "Ha, accuracy isn't truth. It's all a matter of suggestion. You don't mind if I knit while we're talking?"

Aristide gazed at the yellow floppy piece of knitting. "Incidentally, what became of Fuzzy's sting?" she said.

Brenda's needles clacked and darted. "Don't you remember? We dropped it in Book Three *Fuzzy Bee Takes a Bath*. It seemed unnecessarily violent. And besides, the children were inclined to confuse it with - you know what. I'm so dreadfully allergic to stings, by the way." She shuddered.

She knitted on like a bee cleaning its forelegs. A steady buzz of contentment issued from her as she worked. Aristide lit a cigarette. She regarded the back of Brenda's head and carefully blew voluminous wafts towards the round little skull.

As Brenda absorbed the smoke, the clicking grew less fierce and Brenda's fingers moved more slowly - until, at last, the knitting fell from her grasp. Aristide moved over to the book-case and took down Morse and Hooper's *Encyclopedia of Bee-Keeping*. She had purchased it in the early days when she fatuously imagined she ought to "research" her nasty little tormentor. Her eyes flipped over to the section on the introduction of the queens to the hive. "One method," she read, "is by dunking a queen in honey ...", she smiled. Apparently it was not likely to be successful between April and September. She shivered at the summer heat outside. Her eyes followed the text: "Queens late in mating should be destroyed." She looked down at the sleeping Brenda. Her unraddled face was innocent of the cares of husbands or childbirth. The same cherubic smile that had implanted Fuzzy's face on a million suggestible minds and chained Aristide to Fuzzy Bee. Well, she would have her bees, plenty of them. Aristide picked up the yellow knitting.

"My God," she breathed softly, "I do believe it's a pollen bag!"

She stubbed out the cigarette, took the pot of honey from the table and let it drip slowly over Brenda's slumbering smile. Then she opened the door and all the windows. The sunshine gleamed and poured like warm butter over the hives outside. First one bee, then another made its way indoors and hovered over Brenda before alighting to sample the sticky sweet confection they were denied within the hive. In a few minutes Brenda was swarming with creatures anxious to pay their respects to their drowsy new queen. When Brenda finally awoke to scrape them off, Aristide could fly out of their busy little world for ever.

Tell Me About Pierre

It's not as if it actually *was* adultery. The doctor leaned back. "Now - come on ! That's not what I call *adultery* , Mrs Mathers!" He started to grin. "Just dreaming about it!"

It was Emily's turn. "The dream was so vivid." His mouth remained open, poised in disbelief. She paused, then she sighed spaciously into her flowered lap. The doctor put on his kindly expression. Menopausal? Early fifties. The awkward age.

"I want you to undersand," she began again, quietly, "that I've had this dream several - many-times. I didn't come to waste your time."

"Perfectly all right. It's past three. I've no calls - as yet. And there are no patients waiting." He tried to picture her husband. Edward. City man. Lion's profile. An accountant. Bristly moustache and pressurized cheeks. Then he thought about the glass of whisky he always awarded himself after surgery. He could actually feel it palpating his throat lining.

"It comes about three o' clock in the morning, regularly. It wakes me up and it wakes my husband. It's as if it -" she faltered and loosened her lemon organdie scarf, "-It's as if he - was coming back to torment us."

The doctor smiled. "That's fanciful ! You already said that the incident happened in your youth. That it was innocent. Now, I could give you some pills - break the sequence. Or - I could refer you on. Psychopathic disorders aren't my thing... actually - " he gave his we-all-have-silly-thoughts-at-3am-smile, " - I think you should let Nature..."

Her eyes dropped to the large embroidered flowers on her knee. She had already dismissed the doctor. She made all her own dresses, and always had difficulty balancing a pattern as big as this.

Next day in the brown varnished cavern of the Church of the Blessed Virgin, Father Doonan decanted his minty breath at her through the grill of the confessional. He was trying to give up smoking again and the mints worried him. They were at once replacement therapy and a disguise for the occasional cigars which kept him going. She listened to his low brogue, caressing and waxen.

"You cannot repent" my child, unless you have done something really bad."

"Yes, father."

"It was postcedent to the marriage?"

"No. It was before the marriage. But it wasn't carnal sin."

"And you say you only dream about this - phantom?"

"Many times."

"And do you wish to sin in your sleep?"

"I sometimes feel tempted."

"You must wrestle with the torment. Every day we go through the torments the cloven hoof stamps on our minds. We must fight our daily battles."

Emily Mather caught the grinding sound as he popped another mint into his mouth. Her hand went to her throat and she fingered the beads hanging there. Large, shiny and assorted, they were like coffee and cream dragees in the milky lucence of a hundred candles.

"Duth thith man exith?" Father Doonan asked.

"Does?"

"This man exist?"

"I think he might still live, Father."

"The fight is with yourself, my child. Go in peace."

Father Doonan rearranged his cassock to show that further speech was pointless She rose to allow another penitent to take her place.

"Thank you, Father."

Outside, the splash of sun on her face chased the gloom she always felt from talking about it. She was quite used to talking with professional men. There was only one left to explain it to. She would tell Edward tonight. Somehow she felt that it was a problem to be shared; that she wasn't entirely responsible. The Open University tutor had revealed in the last Summer School the potency of Freudian symbols in our culture. The sexual imagery of art was apparently all-enveloping. Even in the kitchen, hardly Edwards domain - her eyes flitted from voluptuous egg-timer to phallic pepperpot, and leapt from penetrating flash of knives to the deep womb-orifice of the hanging salt pot. It was like when somebody had forever ruined the Fingal's Cave Overture for her by singing it to the phrase "How lovely the sea is ! How lovely the sea is !" An afternoon's baking was hardly possible without encountering physical, genital, erotic signals. She turned down through the shadows of Monks Wynd and went into the Abbey Bistro. She richly deserved the reward of a custard vanilla slice and a cappucino.

"You think he might still live there?" Edward said as they sat in the car by the bay. He screwed up his eyes and looked down over the peninsular. The sea was half in. That meant it would be high by about six o' clock. He wondered, bearing in mind the angular slope of the beach, if the neap tide could float the cobles lying up near the wall? Emily Mather looked over the cliffs. She saw the sweep of the bay like a gathering curve of necklace drawn round the neck of a chilled woman. The sea sent white pinches of foam to nip and fret at the sand's edge.

"If I didn't know you better I'd believe you've brought us on this holiday just to hunt him out !" Edward laughed at his own preposterous suggestion. Emily traced out a crease on her skirt. Although they had been to the Gower before she had never dreamed of meeting Pierre here. Surely he had moved by now. All the same, it could be a pilgrimage of exorcism as well as a holiday. This was where their 'incident' had taken place, in his parents' big house on the hill.

She thought of the opulence of that house, then of their two-star hotel with its impossibly small waste paper basket with the tassels. Of the painted-over rust on the balcony, the green dripping moss in the rockery.

She felt sorry for Edward. He was part of the story. Part of the reason she had come here. For herself, the physical part of their marriage had only held her interest as a kind of disability which afflicts half the human race. That part of their relationship was all in Edward's ordered mind.

It seemed that Pierre had come to stand between them, a ghostly promise of something that had never really happened. All those years ago they had made a pact to sleep together without touching, a Tristan and Isolde. Hardly out of the sixth form, they had aspired only to a union of minds and she had enjoyed the almost holy feeling like a paralysed snake, vulnerable, unviolated, a passion promised and unfulfilled. Now he had returned in the night to tempt her again, to taunt her with the fantasy of consummation, perhaps here, in the Gower, it could be laid to rest. She had only to see him again and the spell might be broken. It was a long shot. He couldn't possibly still be here.

She had read all about the change of life in books written by professional men. She knew how these things happened. These men described the process in beautiful technical detail. Finall, it was her problem. That was why she could not bring herself to explain to Edward, nor to the doctor, nor to Father Doonan. Her relationships with all men had been peripheral, half-suggested, incomplete.

"I'll take a turn on the beach. Will you have far to walk?" Edward was making it easy. He was already half way out of the car.

"He lived up here. In the old town, with his family. It's quite near, I think, further up the hill. I'm sure they will have left years ago."

"Was it his father who was French?", he asked suddenly and politely.

"His mother was French. His father was posted to the French Embassy. That's where they met." As she said this she felt like an authority recalling history to which she had a proprietary right.

Edward was merely being polite. Why did he bother with all these details?

"I take it they were all Catholics?"

"Yes."

"Well, don't ask me to come," he said a little irritably. "I can't stand reminiscences when I'm not involved".

She watched him go down the hill. A sensible, upright man. She could read the set of his back, the pretended indifference he projected for what she was doing.

Up the hill she didn't notice the autumn chill and the hair-fine rain. It was too steeply tiring to feel sensations on the skin. The houses were individual and different. Mournful, sombre dream dwellings, but dignified in their commanding position over the raw-red developments below. Soon she entered an old ashlar-clad world where, in the heaving cobbled streets, ferns and grasses forced apart the ancient dressed stones. Here and there brash gouts of new brick shored up imminent collapse. A bright plastic container casually mocked between grave stone mullions.

She thought back over thirty Summers as she bent her back up the hill. The last time she had come this way the youthful muscles in her calves had pushed her effortlessly upwards. Pierre and she had come up swinging carefree, hand in hand, not knowing whose hand was pulling or pushing the other's. His face was ivory in the May sunshine. And the hair she loved to comb stood like gold coins on his head.

Once in the house, as his parents were still in Paris, they had swiftly and self-consciously prepared the bed. The bedroom, she recalled as in the dream, was hung with grey-green watered silk brocade and the air was misted with a dusty powerful perfume. He had brought his university books up from the stone basement. He unpacked the Rousseau volumes which they read in the firelight, the Catholic apologists, and the crowd of pre-Revolution dramatists. She remembered only Racine and Voltaire from her schooldays. But it was enough to defer to the mystic French

The Singing Men

heritage to which he and his mother, and this house, held the keys.

They lay there, naked, side-by-side, little fingers snake-linked. Even in sleep they hardly touched. Eventually their fingers parted and stole back to the sleeping coils of their keepers.

She strained up the last incline. Her leg muscles pulled like taut catapults. Her head bent forward and the heavy beads swung on her breasts. She stopped. The next house above announced itself like a mischievous trumpet. It stood sulkily, leaning against the side of the hill, as if it had waited too long for her. Even the dream garden. It foamed with rank seeded grasses.

It was undoubtedly the same house. Even the doorbell had a high French lilt. It was opened in a minute by a robust middle-aged woman. She knew instantly they were still there.

"Is this Mrs Duerden's house?" She didn't know why she asked for his mother. Mrs Duerden had not figured in her dream.

The woman nodded. She wasn't wearing a uniform or any visible sign of servitude.

"I'm Emily Mather, an old friend of the family. Is Mrs Duerden at home?"

"Mrs Duerden never goes out nowadays". She motioned Emily to enter as if conferring a privilege.

The passageway from the front door was dark and saturated in a plum colour. It opened onto a small receiving hall hung with a gilt Empire chandelier.

"Mrs Duerden is in the snug. We call it the snug. It's the only part of the house she can afford to heat as much as she wants. I hope you don't find it too hot." The maid paused before the door, her hand an inch above the knob. "Mrs Duerden is a very old lady. She went blind many years ago, long before I came. Cataracts. they said. Must make allowances.

Emily caught the cloying scent of cachous as she brushed past the hangings near the door. To one side dropped the circular basement stairs.

"Curtains are to keep out the draughts," the maid explained. "She always insists on a coal fire, even in Summer."

She opened the door and a firm stroke of warm air wrapped itself round   Emily's face. The fire in the grate flashed its greeting as the flames chased up the chimney.

In the corner sat a hunched figure as in a sepia photograph. The golden light lit up the room which appeared to be covered in browning cream paint. The firelight glinted where it showed between pictures ranked on the walls.

Mrs Duerden rose to meet her as the maid melted through an opposite door, pulling in a cold blast of air from some room beyond. Emily hurried forwards to shake hands. She tempered her grasp when she touched the frail folds of skin. They clung to her like damp leaves of *papier poudre*.

As Mrs Duerden stirred her dressing-gown Emily caught the aroma of - what was it? Oil of almonds? Attar of roses? She let the hand lie for a moment in her own; a small cage of fossil bird bones.

"You may not remember me, Mrs Duerden. I'm Emily Mather. It was over thirty years ago. I was a friend of Pierre's. From the university".

It took a second or two, then: "My dear! Pierre? At the university? A long time ago. Mather?" The French accent teased the name, but there was no recognition. Mrs Duerden looked fixedly past her left shoulder and Emily remembered her blindness.

"Emily Grant. That was my name then. You probably don't remember? I was lucky to find you still here."

Mrs Duerden motioned her to sit.

"I came to Paris once with Pierre. And I stayed in the embassy."

The old lady, nodding, a doll on a weighted base.

"And I stayed here for a night. In this house. You were in Paris."

Mrs Duerden circled her thin arm to encompass the house. Her lips pressed in a grimace. "It is cold, this house," she complained. "It is too gross."

Emily knew this would happen. It might be best to cut the whole thing short. The door opened and the maid entered with a tray of coffee and some tiny madeleines.

"My husband and I are on holiday in Swansea. I dropped - called - in to see if you could give me Pierre's address."

A smile crossed the old lady's face. "Pierre! *Quel petit copain!* That one! I think I remember you. You - and Pierre. Well, my dear, it was a long time ago. And now you have lost him." She spoke with relief that such marionette games were things of the past for all of them. Emily's lips tightened. The old woman couldn't see her. She had met this attitude in the old, in her own mother, before the end. The delicate line between beguiling politeness and pointed cruelty. Like children they could not help revealing their innermost thoughts.

"Pierre is married and living in the Auvergne, my dear. They have two children. It is a pity -"

"Yes?" Emily looked hopefully at the blank eyes.

"It is a pity that you have missed to see them. They, too, are on holiday. They have left from here to go to Ireland yesterday. You are unlucky once more."

"I am an unlucky person," Emily said as flatly as possible. Mrs Duerden shifted her fingers till they grazed the coffee tray. Emily guided her hand to the cup.

"There is no need. I have lost my sight since twenty years. I know every object. As long as I do not stray from this room."

"I am sorry I missed Pierre."

"You must see my photographs now that you have come." Mrs Duerden bustled efficiently to a desk near the wall.

"I should have liked to have seen his children, and his wife."

"You shall see them all." She threaded her way expertly between the tables round their chairs to bring several large albums. The aroma of the peculiar scent was almost stifling in the heat of the fire.

"Here." She held out the albums in the direction of Emily. "You shall brighten the day of an old woman. You shall see his life from the day you left him. And I shall relive some happy moments."

She spoke precisely with her elegant accent, and recomposed her lips in a hanging smile after each statement.

"Tell me what you see there," Mrs Duerden commanded.

The pages turned stiffly with the photographs. She felt her head dizzy as she saw Pierre.

"Is that how you remember, my dear?"

"Just how I remember. It is him, exactly."

The old lady leaned back chewing a cake, evidently satisfied.

"Here is one with his wife."

"Ah, Simone!"

Emily rapidly calculated the date under photogrpah. Not two years after Pierre had left her.

"Tell me how he is looking!" Mrs Duerden rocked in her chair. Emily felt flushed. The fire seemed to lead a life of its own, never seeming to burn any less.

"Well, he is very handsome. The photo shows him as very young - as I knew him."

Emily felt her mouth flood with saliva. It would be impossible to go on. She turned the pages rapidly. Mrs Duerden listened for the rustling of paper.

"Please. You must continue. Is there some photograph you do not recognise?"

There were more albums of the family. Black and white gave way to colour prints. A changing, ageing family. The figures no longer fitted together in an intimate group. Distances between the subjects increased like birds strung out on a wire. Their attitudes were attenuated. Their eyes had sobered and their faces calloused. Emily turned the pages. The two daughters had grown gangly, their soft limbs showed the rivalry of bone and muscle. At the same time Simone had acquired, like many Frenchwomen, a fatigued kind of elegance, as if she wished it were all over and done with.

"Tell me about Pierre," Mrs Duerden said. "Tell me how he is looking."

Emily stared at the page. Pierre had changed as often as the Fates decree. From those they endow with early beauty, they often withdraw it later.

"Pierre is looking very masterful."

She turned the pages. Thirty-five. Forty. Forty-five, and into his fifties. Pierre had sacrificed golden youth for complacent middle-age, His hair had crept furtively to the sides and back, giving his bald head a ruthless exposed look. It was clear that neither his razor nor Gallic fastidiousness had kept pace with his jowls. They now hung porcine and blue, reprovinng and gross.

Emily looked at Mrs Duerden, at her eager parted mouth.

"He has grown much. He is mature," she said.

She gazed at Pierre's bursting stomach, concealed by the suit, but cruelly protruberant in his relaxed moments. It was hardly possible she could have kissed those lips, sensual, almost turned back on themselves in a clownish, rubbery way.

She looked across at Mrs Duerden. The blue veins on her neck strained as her ears cocked to hear the words she craved.

"He - Pierre - he looks very dignified - as a proper French papa should."

"Pierre is very respectable," Mrs Duerden said eagerly. "Pierre is *comptable*."

"Comfortable?"

"*Comptable*." The old lady waved her hand impatiently. "Book-keeping."

Emily looked again. She thought that all accountants were lean and wiry, like Edward.

Mrs Duerden leaned forward, hungry for some more charitable words.

"If you could see him" said Emily, "you would think him most handsome. You must be very proud." She stared at the ugliness of Pierre. He would now remain forever a fleshless chimera - half-memory, half-photograph.

Mrs Duerden sank back, radiant and happy. The flames in the fire flickered and crawled. The heavy scent of perfume was shifted by something more acrid and unpleasant. The door opened and the maid came in for the coffee tray. She stopped and sniffed the air.

"Goodness, Madame," she said, blushing, "it's time for your bath."

Her eyes motioned Emily away and her shoulders shrugged at the incontinence of the old. Her strong arms braced under the the old lady's armpits as she lifted her from the chair. Emily gave one last thankful press to Mrs Duerden's hand and signalled her way to the door.

Outside the rain had stopped. Walking down the hill was nearly as tiring as walking up it. She looked back and the house seemed quite normal as it slotted back amongst the others.

Edward was already back in the car, fiddling determinedly with the starter.

"Well," he said at last, "are you going to tell us about Pierre?"

"Nothing much to tell. He's gone on holiday to Ireland."

He looked at her sideways. "Was there ever really anything between you two?"

"If you mean did I sleep with him - we didn't do that sort of thing in the fifties. Not unless you were really fast."

She glanced at him to see if he was looking smug. And she felt tired, drained and sleepy. She let his hand rest on her knee. Then she turned in the seat and kissed him, looking clear into the stone pits of his accountant's eyes whilst she did so.

Death of a Gasholder

In between A Levels and Uni I decided to visit the real world. If my dad hadn't been unemployed I could have gone round the world for a year. As it was, I joined Dodger's demolition gang and the Halifax Building Society. In that order.

Dodger was the gaffer and he never bought a pint until Friday payday. All the other days he sat with his cadged glass of Brickie's Dew in front of him. The gang took it in turns to buy it on the other four days. If he went to the lav he would take out his glass eye and pop it in his beer glass. It would crouch at the bottom winking up at us. A bottled cyclops. Dodger knew none of us would fancy a sip with his eye watching us. I told Dodger I was going to take English Lierature, and he nodded and apparently forgot the remark. I never dreamed of the effect it would have on the gang.

Dodger had recruited them to demolish the gasholder when they were just disillusioned, hippo-necked, beer-bellied artisans hanging about the job centre. I soon found out why he had included a token student. Underneath the box-like construction of his frontal lobes there lurked an old-fashioned Tawney socialist. As he explained on the very first day, his good eye flashing menacingly, the working man was not respected whilst he inhabited a cultural vacuum. I began to see where I came in.

Jobs were hard to get. And it didn't take us long to fall in with Dodger's vision of the basic philosophy underlying the demolition of a gasholder. There was little Dumper who could spin his truck round (admittedly with the engine warmed to operating temperature) to catch a playfully thrown brick before it could hit the deck. Compo Baines, arms like hydraulic jacks, could keep a dozen brickies going with hand-mixed mortar. Taff 'The Trowel' Jones, a redundant shop steward from the old days of the unions, and Shoddy McDowell, who could lay a hundred breeze blocks in an hour with (as he liked to explain) a following wind. All these homely trades had been humiliated in this industrial desert. Instead of creating things we were demolishing them, beginning with the gasworks.

"I expect you think," said Dodger, addressing them in the vaults of the Teeming Ladle for the first time, and indicating me, "I expect you think that poets are pale, pigeon-chested youths with long sloping fingers, unhealthy hair and limp wrists?" Dumper attempted to intervene, not recognising a rhetorical question. Dodger put him down with a scowl, and put his hand on my shoulder affectionately. "Be that as it may, Peter here is a poet, and you lot are a collection of muscle-bound wreckers. We all have to learn from each other. By the time this Summer's over, he'll have muscles, and you'll have a taste for poetry. Let me give you a sample."

I looked around at the drawn, stubbled faces. Taff was already shaking his head disbelievingly. Compo and Shoddy simply stared. Beerwise, Dodger had already levied what amounted to a new variant on the Danegeld. Poetry was simply an outrageous flourish of his terrible power of engagement and dismissal.

Dodger then proceeded to give us an example of what he had in mind. It was entitled *The Headless Gas Meter Inspector*, and this piece of doggerel became a sort of work chant as we swung our sledgehammers that first week. Dodger had a new one for use the second week, *The Ballad of South Bank Brewery*. It was an innocuous piece about a plasterer who got accidentally locked in a brewery over the week-end, and triumphantly fought off a hail of bullets when the police tried to restore production, until the following Monday. There were various risible references to him being 'plastered' and to having died as he lived, drunk as a fiddler's bitch. There were several polite titters.

Dodger named us the Yeller Wellie Poets and described as us a macho grass roots literature squad. I was looked upon as a youthful fountain of knowledge and inspiration and an example to them all. I had already marked out Taff for *Under Milk Wood*. Betjeman, perhaps, for the more urban bucolic Dumper. It seemed to be getting serious when one evening Dodger introduced into the vaults a fat little chap wearing a collar and tie and a natty gent's suit.

This anti-prole attire had already provoked the frowns of several customers, and El Gringo, mine host at The Ladle, advised us to use another room. In the upstairs parlour, Natty Gent's Suit explained that the Council, far from pressing poll tax charges, was anxious to give us £100 to finance a community arts initiative. Dodger had set the whole thing up. NGS explained that it was a 'kick-start' grant and that the group mustprovide matching funds to get it off the ground. Dodger clarified this later, saying that it meant we could get our beer half-price.

That evening we were formally constituted as the Yeller Wellies Poetry and Drama Group. I was elected Minutes Secretary. Dodger reserved for himself the critical post of Treasurer until he got to know his fellow committee members better. Everyone was committed to write at least five verses of *The Ghost of Scrapyard Sam* - a poetic happening for street theatre in fifteen cantos. As NGS had explained, the public house was the natural home of the lost art of the ballad.

At the same meeting certain other mundane bureaucratic minutiae were hammered out and minuted. No wives or girl-friends present on composing evenings. No cheating with stuff that didn't rhyme. No more drinks booked before the previous round had been properly supped.

Some of the Group began by regarding it as a sort of anti-perk, a penalty for being employed at all. Some said the Group was held together simply by the arts grant, coupled with the discount Dodger got from El Gringo for bulk drinks for the Group and the promised audience - which reduced the price of a pint to farcical levels. Yet somehow Dodger had got their wick alight.

NGS came to see the first rehearsal of *The Ghost*. Dumper concentrated on the transport aspect of carting scrap to the venue. Shoddy furnished the costumes and Taff would check out the political dimension of the performance. The small man perspired freely and muttered something about 'real people' and 'cultural regeneration'. His briefcase quivered visibly when Dodger's eye thudded down to the bottom of his glass.

Events moved swiftly. In no time, it seemed, Dodger had captured the imagination of the Council, got our pictures in the newspaper, was flaunting himself on local radio, and even began teaching an evening class in Creative Writing, which paid a lot better than shift work. Taff claimed that he was drifting away ideologically from his old marrers and pandering to the long-haired middle-class literary elite. Dodger pointed to the increasing subsidies devoted to a pint of El Gringo's Brickie's Dew.

Then, as if to further disarm his critics, Dodger came up with another idea. Why not turn *The Ghost* into something more than a *piece d'occasion*? Like making it the centrepiece of an arts festival based on the Teeming Ladle? Compo worried about the drain of funds from the kitty to inessential props and booking fees. Dumper thought they were getting too big for their wellies. Taff shook his head and needed time to think.

Dodger produced his trump card at the next meeting. In an extraordinary exercise of chairman's perogative he revealed that in secret talks with the Council (aka NGS) he had consented to host in the Festival an African poet on a visiting fellowship.

The appearance of Mungo Chimbaya amongst us caused something of a culture shock. Poets were still regarded by some as pale of countenance and limp of wrist. Mungo was black and squat. Coloured people, Compo claimed, ate poppadums and sold anoraks in Stockton Market. Not that the regulars were racist. Every one of them could have a good laugh at a racist joke without it necessarily turning nasty. At the same time, we were on trial. It needed only a sudden spark and all the goodwill they had built up with the Council would be gone, along with the grant. Many felt they were treading on a knife's edge, and it would have been better to have booked a fisherman's choir from Redcar. Or even someone from Darlington, playing the flute.

Beyond this badinage, the Yeller Wellies were understandably tense about their local reception. Already there had been friction with the drinkers down in the public lounge who, near closing time, had made frequent forays up the back stairs to dislodge what they colourfully referred to as "them Lambrusco-quaffing poufters."

Dodger had booked the introductory reading for a Friday night. It being giro day, The Ladle was slightly more crowded than usual. El Gringo had insisted that it take place in the upper room, away from the good-natured jostle in the bar. The meeting started at 6pm. Dodger hoped to charge a nominal sum at the door, calculating that he would cash in on giro day and that the bar would be crowded for the semi-final of the World Cup later that evening. The reading would be a sort of warm-up for the football. Unfortunately, their minds were focussed elsewhere,

The Council man was there drinking half-pints. Mungo arrived at a quarter past, by which time the dedicated poets were trying to imitate a crowd by waving their arms and talking rapidly for the benefit of NGS.

Dodger hurriedly rescheduled the start to 7pm to allow the Yeller Wellies to drag in their girlfriends and the odd whippet. But numbers were still low, and everything pointed to a dreadful evening and terrible cash flow problems.

Dodger was depressed, "This lad's come all the way from the African jungle to read his stuff. Some of it's in the original Swahili. It's not good enough!"

We all felt for him. Mungo sat, a small dark figure, with a lemonade in front of him because of his religion, fingering his latest slim volume, courtesy of the Arts Council, looking as bright as a tinker's whistle.

Dodger was forced to start his lengthy introduction, dwelling on Mungo's childhood, the harshness of native initiation ceremonies, his several marriages, tribal guerrilla warfare, and his eventual obsession with poetry. It was difficult to hear him because of the swelling roar from downstairs. Then Mungo stood up.

He regretted that he was unworthy, and he came from a country small in people but large in area. He apologised for spending so much Arts Council money and that he was barred from partaking of the wine of the country. He looked round the tiny gathering.

"It is a thousand pities that more people cannot come out of their houses to hear this literature. But I know that there are many gathered in the room downstairs waiting for their great sporting ceremony. We should tap into one another's culture. I know that Mr.Dodger has arranged for us to finish at eight to view the football. This I am most anxious to do".

Dodger smiled weakly.

"Poetry", went on Mungo, "should be the right and the possession of all, not a particular minority". Taff nodded his head sagely. Compo looked severely at the ceiling. It was a hot night and the perspiration stood out on Mungo's head like steam on a coffee bean.

The Singing Men

Dodger shifted uneasily in his wellies.

"I would like", Mungo said, "with Mr.Dodger's permission, to invite some of our brethren from downstairs to tap into our present joy."

He beamed at us all."Without payment!" His eyes twinkled roguishly, he put down his lemonade glass and before anyone could raise a warning hand, he sped swiftly through the forest of empty tables and slipped down the stairway. Dodger hurtled after him.

We have to rely on Dodger's version of what happened next. Mungo first tackled a clump of welders just off the afternoon shift, and looking just a fraction blacker than Mungo himself.

Maradona had just come on the pitch, and the welders' attention was divided between him and Mungo's enthusiasm for the African literary tradition. The low murmur of discontent at Mungo's intervention was amplified by the state of inebriation of most of the Ladle's customers. Mungo stood on a table and was about to expound the cultural significance of papyrus writings in Nubia when a building worker seized him roughly by the throat. Much later Dodger explained to the final extraordinary meeting that the worker had just finished a trying shift on the local council estate, where his day's work stood every chance of being demolished by the local toughs before he could turn up to finish it tomorrow.

The building worker had given a short resume of his opinion of the relative merits of soccer and poetry. There was a further coda in which he compared the genetics of the African and Nordic races. As Mungo was hoisted into the air, the building worker was heard to remark with surprise that a body so small as Mungo's could weigh so much.

The next incident tested the difference between lifting a hod of bricks all day and undergoing guerrilla training in a jungle setting. The brickie found himself gripped in a sinewy bunch of battle-hardened fives, and struck between the eyes by the frontal lobes of Mungo's forehead - a blow he was to liken, in the reflective comfort of D Ward, to the skull of a punch-drunk Texas Longhorn. Friends of the fallen bricklayer removed his body to a respectful distance, and Mungo actually collected a small troupe of open-mouthed drinkers. Under the impotent gaze of El Gringo he marched them upstairs to where the rest of us were silently waitiing. We listened to Mungo reciting his native poems with a sort of stunned reverence, for the rest of the evening. Dodger still had his head in his hands when the police arrived.

Dodger had to render an account of total attendance figures on his Council renewal grant form. He counted in the downstairs crowd on the grounds that they could have been seated but for a last minute rush. The Council official was in no condition to question the figures, as Dodger had plied him with enough halves to dull his attention.

At the final meeting it was clear that the end of the Yeller Wellie Poets was nigh. El Gringo refused to have the group on his premises again. Dodger was forced to pass a resolution saying that in future no ethnic poets would be invited. This brought a quick withdrawal of grant under the Council's equal opportunities scheme. The remainder of Cash in Till went to augment the sick pay of the unfortunate brickie.

It was the end of Summer. Dodger was devastated. The gasholder had been finally felled and I received my enrolment documents from the University. We all got our cards and P45s. Mungo's European tour was ending.

Before the Poetry Group broke up, our last vision was of Mungo Chimbaya standing on the greasy local station platform waiting for the train. Taff, Shoddy and Compo were there, jobless and shivering in the misty exhalations of factories just starting up. By chance I was catching the same train to the University campus.

"So it's Africa tomorrow then?" asked Dodger conversationally.
"Yes", said Mungo. The blue bulge was beginning to fade on his forehead. "Back to civilisation, my friend". He looked down the line in an abstracted way as if he feared the train might not come. Then he said, "Tell me, Mr Dodger, do English people become violent when they tap into poetry?"

Dodger shuffled his shoulders under his donkey jacket. "Dunno," he grinned. "I expect it gets worse the further up North".

"It is interesting. In my country we tell the poems of the ancients when we have feasting and drinking. There is never fighting".

Dodger thought for a bit. "But you have wars? Tribal wars?"

"All the time", said Mungo calmly. "But they are about land and grazing and water rights".
"Well, you see," said Dodger, who prided himself on his grasp of history, "We did all those things in the eighteenth century. We've moved on since then."
"I think perhaps war is necessary to man and that poetry will not unite peoples in peace."
"Neither will the World Cup, boyo," said Taff dismally,

Mungo looked down the line again as the blue and yellow pencil of the train poked into the station. I sat by him all the way to Birmingham where I changed. Neither of us spoke much. At least, both of us were richer in experience, and speeding forward to a promising future.

The Launching

Karen looked down at her da as he slept on the sofa. He snored like an eruption of the soul, and his legs sprawled still encased in the soiled working trousers. She had managed to get his coat off, but his weight had defeated her. A sense of propriety stopped her removing his trousers even though she knew he wore long johns underneath. A daughter's duty went only so far. If the sofa got stained it was her mother would make a fuss.

She wasn't disgusted when she saw him like this. The welders drank more than any of the shipyard men. It was dirty, dusty work they said, like coal-mining. You could say the same about cleaning the house.

She lit the gas and listened to the whirr of the kettle. She never put on her outdoor shoes until the last minute, partly to save them, but mainly because she could imagine she was still in bed when she scrabbled her toes in the clips of the hearthrug. And that was another thing. A clip rug in the 80s! They really made them to last.

She shivered in the black-lead light of the room. Starlight rivetted the upper window and from one side condensation shattered the yellow gantry lights from the docks down the street. In the grate the newly-made fire burst from the coal in gasps of white veil and fierce orange jets. A landscape on a distant planet.

She liked this time of day before the hooters began, when she had her da to herself. When things seemed unreal, people could lose their ordinary selves, and the shapes of furniture started to creep out from the walls and corners. The dark could wrap her movements and she could pretend to be a great loitering girl with her pelvis thrust out at the tramps near the school gates, or with her legs dancing witch-high, tangled in her leather skirt.

Her da jerked and his wheezing shifted a pitch. She saw the brown hair in his nose quivering and his tongue stole out over his lips. Stubble had sprung on his cheeks and she remembered when she had shaved him

The Singing Men

when he had the injured wrist. Like the sleepy feeling when you are combing someone's hair.

The kettle jigged on the boil and she brewed a small teapot. It would come out brick-red. And strong - what was it? You could trot a frog on it. With the top of the milk, it was just the way he liked it. And plenty of sugar.

"Do you want tea with your sugar, Da?" she would tease him.

The morning light braced itself more strongly, and furniture pushed through the drapes of the dark. Now she could see even the sepia photographs on the sideboard. Her da seemed taller, but that was because he was slimmer than in his wedding suit. He and her mother were standing to the side of one of those fluted columns with a vase of roses.

She looked at the two figures who seemed to be trapped in the middle of some silly music-hall routine. They were almost ready, if invited, to trip lightly out of the frame and foxtrot on the polished top. She looked away quickly, and they had to stay frozen in the twenty-year giggle of which she was probably the echo.

She thought of her mother ill upstairs, warm, alone and undisturbed. She looked at her da again, on the sofa all night, and marvelled at the consideration of men. And she leaned down, and pushed gently on his shoulder. He stopped snoring.

"Da!" she whispered, "Da!" He stirred. "Time for your shift."

His eyes opened. He stared at her with a boy's frightened look, then at the mantlepiece clock. She stared back, divided from him. He smiled his father's full-to-the-brim smile. She gave him her arm and he slid off the sofa and she felt the pull of his short powerful body, and the smell of yesterday's sweat as he moved.

She put his tea and the cold bacon sandwich in front of him. And she watched him, holding back her distaste as he bit on the bread and sluiced the tea at the same time. He frowned as if he knew her thoughts. Then he grinned like a younger brother.

"When yer gannin' away then, our Karen?" he asked. She held her breath for an instant, suspecting he might know. Then she recovered, and sighed just so much that he could hear. She realised it was one of his jokes. He turned to drink the rest of the tea.

"Don't worry, I shall," she said. "In my own good time."
She cramped her lips thinly before she remembered that her mother did that. "This place is dead. So are the people."

She paused to let it take effect, but he didn't bite. When he looked up again she smothered her dress and carried her hands down over her hips. He started to fill his snap tin. He would soon be out and she would have the last precious moments to herself before she clocked on at the factory. A whistle cut the air, and he was off through the door, the closing drowned by its hoot. She wouldn't have time to make her usual threat to do a flit and leave them both to each other.

She ran to the window to see him go. If she glanced through the window at a certain angle with her cheek pressed flat cold to the glass she could see him nearly to the end of the street. In the evening, when he came back from the docks at six she could watch for him with the kettle just steaming, and have the tea mashed and on the table before he actually stepped over the threshold. If he was late at a union meeting, she could always stare at the hull of the ship as it reached up over the houses. She could measure how much it had risen, week by week, above the derricks.

In the beginning there was nothing but the big yellow cranes striding across the space where the street staggered down to the dock. Then, as work progressed, the bulk of the ship grew, soaking up the sky at the end of the street. As if someone were closing a cupboard door from the inside. It rose and rose, dwarfing the cranes which had fed it; looming over the houses of those who built it.

Her da, when he was sober and not hang-dog tired, was proud of the ship. It was almost finished. He had an eye for craftmanship as if he had lived in another richer life, where there were no cheap and nasty clothes and furniture, like the stuff that surrounded them now.

Sometimes he would bring out the few wedding presents he had kept. Relics of the honeymoon when they had lived it up like a lord and a lady for two days. The photos on the sideboard, strutting in soft focus. The gleaming canteen of cutlery, pristine and foolishly untouched. And the real leather suitcase they had taken to Blackpool. He had the same pride in the ship. No foreign bolt-on jobs for him.

"She'll be out before schedule," he said only yesterday.

"Gaffer promised a bonus if the deck's finished by next week."

His eyes would brighten with a staring look, probably from focussing on the arc all day. Sometimes it seemed that he could only see the ship and missed the houses and the people beneath.

The room filled white with morning and she went upstairs and saw her mother comfortable. Then she slipped into her own room and took the letter from the top of the chest of drawers. She read it again. The awkward phrasing and the Amsterdam address. The name of the nightclub was *Groot Huis*. She wondered what it meant. The letter was dated some time ago, but they promised to hold the job open three months.

She had made a bargain with herself. When her mother got well again, and when the ship was finished, she would go. For weeks she had prepared everything, buying the odd slip, the occasional pair of tights. As much as she could afford at a time. Even things she couldn't really afford, like the lizard-skin court shoes. She hid them in the cheap cardboard suitcase on the top of her wardrobe, and when she lifted the lid to pile up her treasures, she did so carefully, so as not to disturb the dust and arouse suspicion. When the ship was launched, and they could see the sea again from the top of the street, she would be off across the water.

Her mother tapped on the boards above and she went up with some tea. The bedroom was small, and her mother looked lost, foundering in the folds of the double bed which pushed against the walls. It always smelled of wet flannel up here since her mother had decided to become an invalid. She didn't draw the curtains as her mother would still have her teeth out.

She watched her drink, crouching over the cup like a starved hen. It was amazing. Only a few weeks ago, she had caught them at it. Through the crack at the door jamb, she had seen both of them stretched out on the bed, her da's hand in her mother's blouse. She looked at her mother, and felt pity and tension.

"You smell nice Karen".

"A new one. Only came in this week."

"Must have been expensive." Her mother cocked an eye.

"I can afford it. Have you finished your tea?"

Her mother gave her the mug and settled back into the pillows.

"I'll be back about five. Have something for your supper, Liver, I expect."

On the landing she paused to glance into her room. The suitcase sat smugly on the wardrobe top.

The next few days had a sulky dullness. During the daytime the cloud shield had been heavy with the last ice particles from the north. At night freezing spring air tipped into the streets. Preparations for the launching went ahead and the workers' houses were linked with bunting provided at the company's expense. On the day itself the women of the area brought out trestle tables from the shipyard canteen, and laid out the spread an hour or so before the ceremony.

Her case was now almost full. Over the last few days she had bought furiously. She couldn't think of anything she might have forgotten. Amsterdam was only a stretch over the water. She looked at the grey hull leaning over the street end bristling with the burden of its superstructure with nearly the same excitement as her da.

As the time drew near, her mother had suddenly found her feet again and came down to help with the trimmings and streamers. Her da went in search of his pub mates, and they spent the last hours toasting the ship they had fashioned.

She had crammed her purchases into the suitcase and when she tried to lift it from the wardrobe top, it seemed full and it creaked and cracked. She left it in its thickened dust for a while longer. It would need a rope or a strap.

An hour before the launching, the sun split the clouds, as if the company had ordered a new day. She had decided to go in the middle of the ceremony, out of the back door. She would leave a note telling them of her plans, and a letter sent to the personnel manager authorising her unclaimed wages to be paid to her da. Her mother would be tearful and bitter of course and be comforted by da, who would know she had done the right thing. He would gradually bring her mother round to that way of thinking. After a week, when the shock had worn off, she could send a card with a present for her mother and a separate letter for da.

The sun in its height warmed the pavement slabs and flushed colour into the flags and streamers. A few streets away, the thump and skittering of drums was taken up by the triumphant clash of cymbals and belltree. She looked through her bedroom window and smelled the stale dust on the window-ledge and leaned her chin against the sash. The band turned the far corner and marched down their street, a great swaggering resplendent caterpillar. The sun flitted on the instruments, flutes, trombones, cornets; a jester capering on tips of radiance. As they came booming past it seemed as if their faces turned towards her, approving her secret in the bedroom.

When the river of gold and scarlet had passed she heard the sonorous speeches decanted from faraway loudspeakers. They seemed to have taken on distance and to be addressing a world of which she was no longer a part.

By half-past twelve the first cracks and rumblings announced that the spars holding the ship were yielding on either side of the slipway. It seemed like the next minute when the ship had trundled away out into the estuary, a great truant child looking back at the heaving pulsing commotion it had created. A huge section of sky had been painted back at the bottom of the street.

She thought of the ship and of her da, and suddenly remembered what she had forgotten – the cooked meat for his snap the next day. She scurried downstairs and out to the general shop on the corner.

The owner, on the sweets and papers counter, looked even grimmer than usual. He didn't smile, but picked up the afternoon edition between finger and thumb and pointed to an item. His gaze fixed on her face. He still didn't speak, but she followed his frown down to his finger.

SHOCK ANNOUNCEMENT - YARD CLOSURE - UNION FEARS CONFIRMED.

  He nodded at her bleakly, like a prophet. Her eyes grew grimmer than his as she thought of her da, then her mother, then herself. She went swiftly out of the shop, listening as she hurried to the slap of the cheers and shouts against the hard brick houses over by the quayside. The noise from a thousand throats chased from doorway to doorway down the terrace as if they pursued her.

  She let herself in at the back door and ran up the stairs to her bedroom, her tears flowing out of control. She was trembling as she reached up and pulled sharply at the cheap suitcase. Then she stepped quickly to one side as the handle came away in her hand. The contents fell from the broken cardboard, showering her with a cloud of lived-in dust, and she looked down at her new things strewn on the lino. She sank down on the bed, covering her face.

  The hot tiredness of her mind broke into great shards of despair which whirled past as she tried to grasp them. She saw the crook of her mother's fingers, chicken claws, pinching back the edge of the bedclothes; her da's face laughing and frightened by turns; the rich leathered glow of the honeymoon suitcases waiting in the next room.

  She rested until her breathing became calmer, then she bent down and pulled on the high-heeled lizard-skin court shoes and walked down, balancing on the steep stair.

  When she opened the front door the street was a broad pathway out to the shining river. A wind, clean and rigid rocketed out of the blue sail of sky and whipped full in her face.

  She could see the ship standing out in the river. It was unbelievably distant, preening in the sun, waving a gathering plume of steam, as if it had finally wrenched itself from the clinging chains of the dockside, though it was caught in a network of efficient tugs which marshalled it to unseen moorings.

  She went down to the end of the strand where the last high-water mark enclosed riverine streaks of rainbow oil and speckled drifts of sea coal.

  She was calmer. She felt more grown-up, as if she had quickly passed through a reckless phase of childhood. As she stood looking at the ship, the slim heels of her lizard shoes settled almost imperceptibly into the freshly-wetted sand.